The Big O

HJ Bellus

Jasmine —
Never fart
in public
♡ HJ
Bellus

HJ Bellus

Bellus

The Big O

HJ Bellus

Dedication-
To the damn letter O and to women around the world hunting down THE BIG O. May your toes curl with happiness and enjoyment! –HJB

HJ Bellus

Prologue

The Damn Diary

Dear Diary,

Sweats, check. An ample supply of new movies for the weekend, check. A box of powder doughnuts, check. Pedro on my lap gnawing on a rawhide. This is it, my life in a nutshell. I'm a loser with a teaching degree and a wild desire to be swept off of my feet by Prince Charming. Not only do I want to be swept off my feet, I want him to pound me into next Tuesday. He needs to ride me like he stole me and toss my V card right out the window.

For now, it's the damn "Notebook", junk food, and my dog.

Love, O

Chapter 1

Meet The Virgin

"He's way too feminine for my type. I mean, I need a little burp and farts to a man." I take a large bite of my bagel smothered in cream cheese. "He looks like he can shit glitter and then make it rain sprinkles."

"O-livia knock it off. You'll never get laid at this damn rate."

I shrug and talk around a mouthful of bagel. "I'll be the crazy Yorkie woman."

Scout nails me in the shoulder. "Look there, Olivia, give him the sexy stare."

"Ewww, no."

I get that Metro may be for some, but not me. I want the calloused hands and construction worker hat.

"Are you daydreaming again about your rough and tough man?" Scout asks.

"You know the pot roast kind with abs and scruff, that's what I want," I say, washing down my bagel with my favorite diet soda.

"You had that with Lester, Olivia."

A shower of diet soda sprays out my mouth and rolls down both my nostrils, causing a shit storm of a brain ache. "Shut your damn mouth when you talk to me."

"Well, you did," Scouts insists.

"That was a blind date, asshole, and he was nasty. His fingernails were longer than mine and filled with dirt."

"Well there's your manly man, O."

Scout Jones is the only living person on the face of this planet allowed to call me O. She's been my best friend since kindergarten, we've owned matching Easter dresses growing up, and have been by each other's side for years.

When my mom passed away it was Scout and her mom who took me in. I mean my dad did his best, but running his own mechanic shop and grieving the love of his life pretty much used up all of his extra time and energy. It's never easy when you lose your wife to breast cancer and then are stuck with an eleven year old blossoming daughter. Like I said, my dad did his best and made it work with of course, the help of our neighbor, Scout's family.

Dad even eventually got comfortable with buying feminine products and used auto parts to give me the birds and the bees talk. I still have nightmares of a spark plug shafting the shit out of a washer with oil going everywhere. I cringed and I do believe my ovaries even sent Hail Marys to Jesus that day in the shop. When Daddio pulled out a piston and began preaching about the different places boys shouldn't be allowed to stick their wieners in, I ran for it. In fact, it was clocked as the fastest sprint in the history of feared sexed speech sprints.

All I can say and will, to my dying day is thank God for Scout's mom, Lily; she saved me in every blossoming womanly way possible. Scout and I went off to college together a whole whopping twenty-five minutes away from home, went through the teaching college together class by class, and then landed a teaching job back in our hometown.

We've dubbed ourselves "courageous-badass bitches." No shit, we even made ourselves sashes and blinged out crowns. Then proceeded to drink bottle after bottle of Moscato until I pissed myself laughing when Scout got a Cheeto stuck up her nose.

Now, here we sit in our hometown mall doing our best to dodge all of our old classmates and their blossoming families. We're known as the hometown closet lesbians who trade furs at night in their canoes or something like that. Scout dared me to stare at a vagina on the computer screen one night without gagging. I blew chunks and then had nightmares hoping my kitty was prettier than the pounded pussy on the screen.

Let's-be-honest, and set the stage of my real life situation. I'm twenty-four, a first grade teacher, have a Yorkie named Pedro, a goldfish named Fish, have never had sex, or a serious boyfriend, and I'm the town lesbian who pukes when she sees a pussy. Nothing really to be jealous of at all.

"Olivia, woof down your biscuit and let's go splurge on our last day of spring break."

I very kindly flip her the bird and shove the rest of my bagel in my mouth. "You mean max out our Old Navy cards. Don't make it sound so freaking glamorous."

5

"Same thing, bitch. Let's roll."

Scout and I couldn't be any more opposite. Me, jet black, board straight shiny hair, Scout, bouncy beautiful golden locks. And of course to pair with the gorgeous blonde hair, she has long legs for miles and ample curves. I'm short and lie every single fucking time when asked my height. I always pad myself at least a good four inches. My tits are a decent size C while Scout's are perfect and ginormous filling out all of her outfits.

"Scout, I really have enough khakis and skirts from Old Navy to choke an elephant."

She slams her hands over her chest. "You evil, rotten, dirty pot licker. Never say that again."

And we go to Old Navy and then every other department store in the mall. Scout's not shy about maxing her card out and living the American dream of wallowing in debt. I'm a bit more reserved when it comes to money. My dad, always the conservative businessman, taught me well.

"Scout, let's go. We will be late for dinner."

She scurries with her heaping arm full of clothes up to the counter while I tap my foot relentlessly on the cement ground, waiting on her. Every single Sunday we have dinner at her parents' house. My father, George, walks across our backyard and waltzes right through their backdoor with his twelve pack of Miller Genuine Draft beer. We are one very charming knitted ball of oddity type family.

"Your mom is going to kick your ass," I tell Scout as we walk into the fresh spring air of Oregon.

"She'll get over it."

"Last time you were late for Sunday night you got a meatloaf pan to the right eye."

"Mom's getting damn batty in her old age," Scout replies.

We both settle in the car and on cue, my butthole puckers with each yellow light Scout blows through, but she makes it to her mom's house with thirty seconds to spare. I stretch out my fingers, letting the flow of blood return to my knuckles. You'd think after years of Scout's driving I'd be a seasoned pro, but like she tells me, I'm a certified chicken liver pussy.

"Taylor has a cousin and wanted to know if you'd like to double date with us next weekend," Scout announces before we get out of her lime green VW Bug.

"Pass. El No. I mean hell to the fucking no. I've been on enough of your damn blind slash double dates of hell."

"You've seen Taylor; he's smoking hot and this is a blood cousin, so same gene pool." She waggles her eyebrows.

"No, Scout, I'm done with your torture. I'm not dating. Your legs spread easier than melted butter and you love having sausage all up in your taco. Leave me out of it. I have several seasons of *Saved By the Bell* to get reacquainted with."

"So, I'll tell him yes." She fist pumps the air. "Saturday at seven."

"I'll have the liquid shits, bitch." I slam the door, giving up on her desperate attempt to torture me.

"Olivia." I look over to the front porch of my childhood home to see my father clothed in his red plaid button shirt, which he's deemed as his "town and Sunday" shirt.

"Using the front door, Dad?" I ask shading my eyes from the glaring sun.

"Looking for Oscar; that damn son of a bitch escaped again." His right hand is wrapped in a paper towel.

"Did that pecker bite you again?"

"He had a stick caught in his mouth and was choking. He didn't bite me."

"The dick accidentally sunk his teeth into your flesh, right?"

I follow him down the sidewalk, behind him as he hollers out Oscar's name.

"And Olivia, stop with all the dick calling. He's a wiener dog for Christ's sake."

"He's Satan, Dad."

"I like him."

"There's the little, cocksucker." I point to the black villain hiking his leg up on a hydrant.

"Come here, boy. Here, boy, Oscar."

"Jesus, you're nicer to the dog than you were to me as a child." I pat his shoulder, watching his face light up as Oscar stampedes towards him. "You'd throw me a cold hot dog and hoped I survive."

"Like I've always told you Olivia, you can't take a hotdog to a steak dinner." He bends down and scoops up his dog and then wraps an arm around my shoulder as we head back towards our house. "I love you very much."

"I know, Dad." I lay my head down in the crook of his arm. It's always been my safety net, the comfort zone where all my problems disappear. "I just like teasing you."

"I know, you little shit."

Oscar bares his teeth to me and I swear they're stained a light pink.

"That bastard's growling at me."

"He senses evil," Dad chimes.

"Old man has jokes. Go get your beer and let's eat dinner."

Dear Diary,

Do you find it funny that my name is Olivia Olander and I live in Ontario, Oregon and teach school in room one and have never had an O?

Love, O

Chapter 2

Just Say No

Mondays have to be the evil spawn of Satan multiplied by infinity. I'd rather be sitting at home in my yoga pants seeing how many needles I can stick into my palm before screaming uncle than functioning on a Monday morning in an elementary school. All the bold primary colors spiral out of control, causing my head to pound and ache and not even coffee can control the vortex of pain.

"How was your morning?" Scout asks, throwing her Lean Cuisine into the microwave.

"Like a donkey's farting asshole, you?"

"I teach fifth grade; it always smells like farts in my room."

"True dat," I mumble riffling through the newspapers scattered on the table in the teacher's lounge.

Who in the hell even reads the paper anymore? I look up to the other professionals in the staff lounge, three of whom probably taught Fred and Barney how to print with a chisel into stone. They carry flip-phones and still use an overhead projector for every single lesson.

Absentmindedly, I stare at Mr. Voulch, the fourth grade teacher, and wonder if, in his prime, he was the shit. I mean, like real cool and legit and all that snazz. My vision scans over his bolo tie and

I take a minute to admire the glossy tan stone in the center of it. The green stain on his white button up shirt assaults my vision and I stare at it like there's no tomorrow. *Is that a boogery snot stain or pea soup?*

I clutch to Scout's arm, pulling her long torso down to me, so I can whisper in her ear. "I'm going to be Mr. Voulch."

"Uh?" She turns to me.

"He's never been married right?"

"That's the word on the street," Scout replies.

"Fuck, fuck, fuck," I whisper.

"What in the hell is wrong with you?" she asks, pulling her meal out and prancing to the table, not letting her hand get burned by the edges of the hot plastic tray.

I settle next to her, pulling out my peanut butter and jelly and continue to whisper like a ninja.

"That's going to be me. Just look at him. Teaching and never been married and for fuck's sake, look at that stain on his shirt."

"You'd wear a bolo tie?"

"Jesus, Scout that's all you got out of that?" I flop my head down on the table and hold back from pounding my forehead on it. "I'm a virgin and hopeless."

"Mr. Voulch." I hear Scout's voice. "Do you own a Yorkie?"

"No." The sound of paper rustling goes off and then no further conversation.

"See, you're fine, champ. He doesn't own a Yorkie. All is clear."

"I guess I'll go on the date Saturday."

11

"I know. Already told Taylor you would. How am I supposed to teach fifth graders who are just coming into their hormones Geometry? Fuck my life."

"Have you and Taylor had sex?"

"Jesus, Geometry to sex, O. Get a grip."

"You're going to think O, Scout. My damn name is Olivia Olander and I live in Ontario, Oregon and teach at Oregon Trail in room one, so yes, I just did switch the damn topic."

"Have you used that toy I bought you?" Scout raises both of her eyebrows up.

"No, the fucker scared me and I tossed it right back into the package."

"It has a ten volt battery that will zap you into next year."

"I just want a man and the O."

"Quit being so desperate, O, you're too cute for it."

"I'm Asian." I slump back down on the table.

"And that matters because?"

"Because I want to be Barbie," I joke.

"But you have slanted eyes and cute dimples."

"You're right, but I want a man like Jillian has and I want her SUV and picket fence and baby bump." The lunch bell goes off and I stand up. "Oh, and the infinite amount of Os Douglas has given her."

"Douglas has a small dick. I nearly chipped my front tooth on his pelvic bone when blowing him our junior and then he got warts our senior year. That shit's like diamonds...forever. No need to be jealous. Hike those titties up and go teach phonics to the future of our country."

"So inspirational, fuckface," I say a bit louder than intended, while throwing my stuff away.

"You two need a good whipping and about a year's worth of church."

We both turn to Mrs. Jackard, the kindergarten teacher and preacher's wife, and smile.

"God bless," I say before slamming the door to the staff room.

I'm off to save the day, one alphabet and peepee dance at a time.

Dear Diary,

Just another day down. Living the American dream with my Yorkie and...Shit, my life sucks, so I'll keep this shit real.

Love, O

Chapter 3

And The Ovaries Go Wild

"Do you know what you're wearing Saturday night on the date?"

I look up to Scout over a mound of testing data and wonder how her brain only functions on dick and Taylor. They've been dating for nearly three years and he's grown to be a brother to me.

"Um, clothes," I respond.

"You need to spruce up your Mary Poppins look if you're hoping for any Dick In Cider." She air quotes the last part.

"I'm not spreading my legs on the first damn date anyway, Scout. I want to fall in love and all that shit."

"So, you want the whole fairytale full meal deal and not just a side of fries."

"Yep." I check off the last reading speed test and push back from my desk.

"You're getting old enough, you should just fuck around."

"Scout." I send her the warning stare to quiet down.

She never has a filter on, even at school. And even though the students are out to recess, I don't feel comfortable with her language. But she seems to never care and this time is no different as she grabs her crotch and thrusts it towards me.

"You're impossible. I swear my first graders are easier to reason with than you."

"I'll bring the outfit over tomorrow night. I'll be there an hour early with a bottle of wine to get all your cobwebs loosened up."

"Taylor will just pick us up at my place?"

She nods and then adjusts her tits until they're spilling out of the V-neck of her school spirit shirt.

"What in the hell are you doing?"

"Taylor asked for dessert, so I'm sending it to him."

"You're gross."

Before I have the chance to really lay into her, my classroom phone goes off.

"Ms. Olander."

"Hi, your community service employer is here. We are sending him down."

"Okay, thanks." I hang up the phone.

"Getting called down to the office?" She waggles her eyebrows. "Maybe Principal Williams will bend you over her knee and spank you."

"You're dumb. It's the last of career week for our special guests."

"Is it another baker or chef. I'm starving."

"No, police officer."

"Gag." She sticks her finger down her throat. "You need that pastry chef back. I nearly came in my panties over her cream puffs."

"Yeah, they were good until Chandra blew a snot rocket on hers and made me gag."

"You're going to have to work on that gag reflex of yours if you ever intend on becoming a cum guzzler."

"Out." I point to the door and begin walking over to it.

The clatter of happy voices begins to parade down the hall. I greet each smiling face with a high five or hug. I've found no matter how miserable my life is that the bright and bubbling innocence of first graders makes it all disappear.

"Grab a drink and your fruit snack quickly little friends before our final career week visitor arrives."

I continue talking about our visitor for career week, flipping through a PowerPoint presentation of our past visitors from the week and then finally end on the final slide. My little gems all take out their reflection notebook and begin jotting down questions they might have about being a police officer. Then I take a count of how many students think they just might go into the field of work. I pick the mini-teacher of the week to place the tally marks up on her learning objective poster.

It's really a small community of little ants in my room. There are weekly jobs that rotate each week which students love to do. You know, line leader, mini teacher, neat freak, hall monitor and on and on. And then there are the golden tickets they earn when they do their job. It's quite magical around the month of April having them all trained to run like oiled machines.

A knock at the door distracts me from admiring the little minions and how far they've come in just one year from sounding out the alphabet to full-out reading. One of life's greatest miracles that it's happened and I haven't spiraled into a full fledged alcoholic by now.

"Jenni, go ahead and get the door." She's the greeter for the week and very enthusiastic about it as she bounds over to the door, stumbling along the way.

I take a seat behind that very special student, who is a perfect angel when I'm near him. Crazy how that shit works. I laugh in my head thinking he will be very acquainted with the law and not in the working way.

"Class, this is Officer Oren O'Brien," Jenni proudly announces.

I pick up my gaze from the back of Kane's blonde locks and come eye to eye with Officer O'Brien. My gaze locks with his deep chocolate brown pupils and I feel the room grow hotter by twenty degrees. Sweat beads form on my brow. He's tall, lean, dark, and motherfucking gorgeous.

"Hello, class." He nods to the students.

And all I can focus on is his bulging biceps in his dark uniform. For a second, I think this is a practical joke Scout has played on me, sending in a damn stripper to our class. His voice is even downright dripping sexy as he introduces himself to the class. It's hypnotic, sweeping me off into a forest of fairies and sinful sexiness.

"Ms. Olander."

A voice snaps me out of my daydream.

Kane tugs on the hem of my shirt. "He asked you a question."

"Oh, sorry." I put up a force shield over my features as I look back up to Officer Sex on a Stick. "What was that?"

"I was sent in instead of the other officer; is there anything you'd like me to cover with these guys?"

"Oh, uh…" I pull the pencil from behind my ear and nearly stab my own eye out with its sharp point. "Just about your job and why you decided to enter the field. They'll have plenty of questions for you at the end."

A messy bun piled on the top of my head; is that really how I slopped my hair together when Fabio is in my room? My God, he's gorgeous as hell.

"Ms. Olander," Kane whispers.

I ignore him, hoping he'll focus on the officer talking in the front of the room, but he doesn't as he continues to tap my hand and whisper my name.

"What?" I whisper yell, finally giving into him.

"Your headlights are on."

"Uh?"

"Your headlights." He nods with his head.

"Kane, you can't even see my car." I kneel down next to him. "You need to pay attention, okay?"

"Your headlights," he grits out between his teeth and then places both of his bawled up fists to his pecs and springs out both of his pointer fingers.

My face heats up to a sizzling crimson, then gracefully I stand back up, and pretend to admire shoes and sure as shit both of my nipples are standing at attention, poking through the thin material of my school t-shirt.

Boogers, boogers, snot, poop, boogers.

I chant it over and over in my mind, trying to reign in my nipples and clear attraction for the officer. But all I do is make myself gag and try my best to cover it with a coughing fit, forcing down my gagger.

"You okay, Ma'am?" Officer O'Brien asks.

The rich smooth tone to his voice makes my insides quiver, turn liquid, and pool in desire. This man should be cuffed and locked away. It should be illegal to be this sexy and the mere thought of him being a hired stripper sent here by Scout is still active and alive in my mind.

I wave him off and grab my throat, letting him know I'll live and let him continue on. It only takes ten more minutes of him passionately telling my students how he decided to become an officer and why his job drives him to be a better human.

Well, isn't that just the fucking cherry on top of my horny sundae, he's gorgeous, brave, and humble. I feel like attacking him and then slitting my wrists from embarrassment.

"Any questions?" he asks the students.

Rachel, my star student, shoots her hand straight up in the air, waving it wildly. Internally, I fist pump and then straighten my shoulders a bit because she'll make me proud as hell.

"I like your uniform." She starts off her question and then sits a bit higher. "And your badge is super shiny."

"Thank you." He leans forward, reading her name plaque on her desk. "Rachel."

"Do you have a girlfriend?"

He chuckles a bit. "Um, no."

And the silence before the storm hits, knocking me incoherent.

"Neither does Ms. Olander and I think you two would make cute babies."

A wave of giggles from the girls and disgusted groans from the boys rolls over the classroom and before I have the chance to scold her and then crawl under the desk, Officer O'Brien speaks up.

"Why thank you, Rachel, your teacher is very pretty."

And my ass cheeks and the cheeks on my face turn an inferno red from burning embarrassment. Note to self, Rachel will never be line leader the rest of the year.

The officer keeps on answering question and thank God none of it has to do with me. His smooth deep voice lulls me into a trance and before I know it, it's time for the kiddos to pack up, and rush out to the buses.

I finally snap out of my sex induced coma and begin ushering the students out the door, lining up the walkers and bus riders, making sure each little nugget gets on their way. Officer

Awesome Sexy Pants takes up residence on the corner of my desk, crossing his ankles and then his arms over his wide chest.

"Ahhhhh." A loud moan escapes me as I'm in a trance from each of his sexy gestures.

"Ms. Olander, do you need to fart?"

I painfully tear my gaze from the officer and down to Bryan. "What, sweetie?"

"Do you have to fart?"

"No, why?"

"You keep moaning like your belly hurts, Ms. Olander like there's a bad poop built up in you."

"Okay, out! Get along little friends, do your homework, and eat your veggies tonight." I give each one of them a high five on the way out and feel my butthole pucker as I turn to face the sex god who rained down from the heavens.

"Funny little fellows," he says.

His voice is richer than any chocolate I've tasted and drips pure sexiness.

"Oh, they're something." I shake my head and pick up some lonely pencils on the tops of desks.

"So, I'm new in town."

I look up at him and smile. No shit he's new in town, I mean men like this don't prance around Ontario, let alone the state of Oregon.

"My chief sent me down on a last moment whim. Another officer was supposed to come but is down with the flu."

I nod, paying very close attention to him and especially to the thick veins in his neck flexing with each word he speaks. My tongue hungers to dart out, lapping over his delicious skin. I switch the energy of my racing mind to the pencil in my hand, spinning it and gripping it with Hulk strength.

"He'd like to offer your class a free field trip to the department including bus fees and stuff. They'd get the full tour and experience of the department."

Omg. A second chance of seeing him. Omg, Omg, Omg, hamsters begin racing around in my mind. I can wear a sexy-sexy ass dress.

The pencil snaps in my hand, causing a bomb of a sound to ring out through the room. "Oh, we'd love that."

I jump back, startled at my own power of snapping the pencil and try to remain cool, not letting him in on my embarrassment.

"Perfect, here's my card when you're ready to set it up." He waltzes up to me until there are only inches left between us and my headlights are now fully on high beams. It's painful the way my body reacts to him. There have been sexy men in college and I've been to my fair share of frat parties where Greek gods strolled around in sheets, but this man is something else. He's shredding my ovaries one word at a time. He has me ready to sink to my knees and I'll make out with his one eyed monster after talking to first graders. Now, that's a sex god if I've ever encountered one.

"Ms. Olander, would you be interested?"

I'm ready to strip down to my birthday suit and jump into his arms and ride off into the sweet sunset with the man. But instead, I'm flicked in the forearm with the sharp edge of the business card he's been holding out.

"I'll...I'll be in contact." I snag the card from him and then study his tight ass in his dark dress pants uniform, nearly melting into an orgasming pool. "Thanks."

I offer up a weak wave as he turns the door handle of my classroom door. Holy shit, I've never seen that metal as a sex tool. That knob is beyond sexy and I'm ready to saddle up as his fingerprints leave an imprint on it.

Head on straight, Olivia, and quit thinking about how you can dry hump that doorknob.

Then I hear her voice.

"Well, howdy there, Mr. Walking Lady Boner." Scout waggles both of her eyebrows very acrobatically up at Officer Oren as she enters the room and he begins to exit.

Their chests brush each other and as if in slow motion, I soak in my best friend, inventorying every single bit of sexiness of Oren. My feet plant firmly into the hideous baby blue stained carpet of my classroom. I mean, I love Scout like family, but in this moment the gal needs to be bitch slapped hard to the right fucking cheek. I'll slit her with a butter knife.

Oren opens his mouth to let out the words, "Excuse me."

It's clear he heard her greeting when his smile lights up and he has dimples. Ovaries down. Ovaries down. The man is tall, dark, with chiseled features, and fucking panty-melting dimples dancing around his smile.

And on cue, her knees buckle and cheeks flush crimson red. Bitch is getting a butter knife to her neck.

And in true Scout fashion, she salutes him, hollering out Captain Lady Boner and then gracefully slips past him. The next portrait imprinted in my mind is Scout on her knees panting and waving the heat from her face. Me, on the other hand, I sprint for my classroom phone fumbling with the card in my hand. Damn rights, I'll make that appointment taking the little gems on a field trip.

Besides being cuffed and stuffed, there's really not any other option. Although, the thoughts of Officer Oren and stuffing sure do give me the chills.

Dear Diary,

The hottest guy waltzed right into my classroom today. No joke! It looked like he was straight off the set from Hollywood. A young Tom Cruise, but a bit taller with more muscles. Oh my God, it was Tom Cruise on steroids.

It's not like he was there to rescue me and ride off on his white stallion. He was there for career week, lame I know! I'm sure my ovaries imploded. I shall dream of this hunk tonight.

Love, O

PS- Officer Oren O'Brien...fucking Os

Chapter 4

Blind Date Vs. Diarrhea

I've gone over every single excuse in the biggest book of excuses to get out of this damn date and not one has proven to satisfy my wicked best friend. The pukes and shits were solid until she texted back, "Prove it."

"Dammit, Pedro." I chase after my little Yorkie, who has his teeth sunk into my favorite lace bra. It's the one that makes me feel sexy, even though I have no one to feel sexy for.

"You damn dog." I bend over and swoop him up into my arms and just like all of the other times, he nuzzles into my neck and melts my heart. Pedro is the worst behaved dog in the world, but he's just so damn cute. Scout teases me that it sounds like I have a sweatshop in my house because every time she walks up the steps all she hears is a crazy lady screaming out the name Pedro.

I plop down on the couch and begin to brush his hair and daydream. Oh, I've been daydreaming since the second Officer Ladykiller stepped out of my classroom. He invades my sleep, waking me with my own loud moans. I've scoured Facebook and all other social media sites to stalk him. And there's been no such luck. *Maybe I got his last name wrong.*

If I had balls, I'd just march right down to the station, find him, and then ask him out on a date.

As awkward as it would be, I totally would if my lady nuts were intact. Instead I'm brushing Pedro, avoiding getting ready for yet another tragic blind date.

The relationship gods thrive on torturing me. I've been through it all. The hot quarterback in college who had the same IQ as a piece of wood, the nice guy who admitted on our first date that he still drinks his mother's breast milk; yep she's been pumping her titties for years to nourish him, oh and my favorite, the sexy geek who when talked about baby kittens, his loose khakis tented right over thy wiener region.

Vomit threatens to spill out just thinking of the top three worst blind dates and I'm just naming the winners, not all of them. It seems all the handsome, normal, nice guys just want to be friends, hang out, and talk shop to my dad about mechanics and restoring old cars. I'm doomed; I'm pretty sure an evil sex witch cursed my mother's ovaries, never giving me a chance at a normal life.

My cellphone goes off, distracting me from the thoughts of an evil sex witch and butt pirates set out to destroy the universe. My dad's name lights up my phone, making me smile.

"Hey Pops."

"Whatcha doing, firecracker?"

"Just sitting on the couch and brushing Pedro." I cringe just hearing how awkwardly of a nerd I am.

"Nice."

"And you?" I ask him.

"Working late tonight. Business has been good. I picked up another big contract with a local taxi service to keep their cars going."

"That's great Dad." I push Pedro to the side, curling up into a comfortable pretzel on the couch. "You know you're going to have to slow down at some point though."

He chuckles lightly into the phone. "Well, my plan was always for my son to take over the business."

"Well, you're shit out of luck, Pops."

"I wouldn't have it any other way, Olivia, and you know that."

"Dad." I pause, not knowing how or how far to go with this.

"Yeah?" I hear papers shuffling on his end of the line and know I'm starting to lose his full-attention.

"I have another blind date tonight."

"Why do you keep punishing yourself with those? A nice young man will come along."

"And if he doesn't?" I counter.

"Look at your mom and me. She was a mail order bride and me just a kid trying to start his own business, too worried about work to date. We fell in love and had you. Love stories don't all happen the same way, Firecracker, give it time."

A laugh escapes me. "Yeah, true."

My elbow is suddenly being attacked by a very horny Yorkie, "Pedro, knock it off."

I do my best to swat him off without hurting him, but his pelvis is in full humping speed, taking it to my elbow.

"Pedro humping your elbow again?" Dad asks and even though we aren't face to face, I can hear the smile sitting on his face.

"Little fucker, yeah he has a real problem humping elbows. He humps nothing else."

"Olivia, you always make me smile, even in the darkest of moments. Be safe on your date and don't give up on love."

"Dad, will you order me a mail order groom if everything falls through?"

"Jesus, Olivia you're a nut and I love you. Talk to you later."

"Hey Dad, why did you call?"

"Just to hear your voice."

I shrug my shoulders and stick my tongue out to Pervy Pedro. "I love you, too, Pops. Bye."

He hangs up his end of the phone. My dad never says bye to anyone on the phone, claiming he's not going anywhere. It used to piss me off, but now I know it's just one of his little quirks.

I drag my ass off the couch, snag a rawhide for Pedro, and then make my way to my bathroom to get ready for the big night. Pedro lies at my feet, gnawing on his rawhide and growling at my pink toes when I wiggle them in his direction.

I decided on my long hair being left down in loose curls, light make-up, and something not too teachery, which is hard when digging in my damn closet. Finally, I find a cute pair of skinny jeans, white lace blouse, and a black leather jacket to wear. At least this cute and somewhat sexy outfit will shut Scout up. Even feeling a bit adventurous, I slip into some high wedges that allow my hot pink toes to peek out.

Now time to wait and you guessed it, my thoughts flow to Officer Oren. As cheesy as it may sound, his looks should be illegal. That strong jaw line, dark brown eyes, and perfectly trimmed hair nearly melted me that day, but it was something else about him. He was nice and down to earth, answering all the questions for the students with thought and care. He was humble. And one thing I've learned is most guys with killer looks like his aren't humble or nice, but rather self-absorbed pricks.

A pounding on my door causes me to scream and trip over one of my high wedges sailing straight into the floor and I'm sent right back to reality.

"Jesus, O, you dry humping the floor?"

I glance up to Scout, Taylor, and my date staring down at me.

I force myself up on my feet, shaky a bit, but trying to act confident, swooshing my long locks over my shoulder. "I fell."

I grit out the two words between my locked jaw and fake smile. Then enters Pedro into the crime scene of blind date gone wrong. He belts out a combination of yips and growls, baring his teeth at the new company and then very gracefully lifts his leg to pee.

"Pedro," I scream bolting forward and once again tripping on my sexy wedges, which are now more like suicide shoes. It's too late as I land in a bit of Pedro's piddle at the feet of my date. Scout's howling laughter deafens me.

Sitting back up on my knees, "I'm so sorry."

Taylor's handsome cousin waves me off with a cute smile. "I'll consider it a warm welcome."

"The little Satan pisses on all new visitors." Taylor pats his cousin's shoulder.

"God, that dog is possessed." Scout begins wiping her tears from her face. "But you falling at your date's feet in a puddle of piss takes the cherry."

I shoot Scout the "I'll slit your fucking throat" stare to shut her up and then very carefully and with my best grace, I stand to my feet.

"Connor, this is Olivia and Olivia this is Connor," Taylor announces.

I go to stick my hand out but think better of it. "Just let me wash my hands real quick and snag you a paper towel for your boot."

Scout is on my heels as I jog towards my small kitchen. Then I'm reminded of the murder weapons that are on my feet and I slow my pace.

"Olivia, we could've won freaking America's Funniest Home Videos with that introduction."

"Shut it." I turn to her and threaten to smear my piss-covered hands over her face.

She throws up her hands in surrender but doesn't stop her fit of giggles.

"It doesn't get worse than that, does it?" I ask, while soaping up my hands.

"He's cute though, right?" Scout waits on pins and needles for my answer.

"He's really handsome," I admit. "So, what's the catch?"

"He may come with a teeny bit of baggage." Scout talks with her hands and I know it's her tell-tell sign that there's more than a teeny bit of baggage.

"Spill," I demand and then flick the dripping water from my fingers into her face.

"His fiancé left him at the altar last month."

"Are you fucking kidding me?" I whisper scream.

"She was a bitch and Taylor's worried about him. He thinks you two could be really good friends and eventually a couple."

"So, I'm the rebound girl?"

"Oh no." She waves me off. "He's screwing the countryside and that's why Taylor is worried about him."

"This little bit of 411 would've been nice to know before." I poke her in the chest.

"C'mon, O, just give it a shot."

"Well, what choice do I have now?" I rip several sheets of paper towels and walk back to the living room, trying to ignore Scout's pleas as she chases me.

"Here." I hand them to Connor. "Again, I'm so sorry."

"No worries." He shoots me a smile and bends over to dry off his boots.

I'll give it to Scout that he's super handsome with his sandy blonde hair, bronzed skin, and killer lean body.

"Just give it a shot," she whispers as we leave my apartment.

I do the only thing a common sensed girl would do and that's sending an elbow to my best friend's gut. Her moan of pain makes me smile. When the spring air assaults my face, I make a promise to myself to go into this date with an open mind.

"I hear you teach first grade," Connor adds as he scoots into the back seat of Taylor's fancy ass truck.

I nod and swallow my pride, steadying myself to engage in mind numbing conversation that has to take place in order to meet someone new.

"I am and what do you do?" I smile and make eye contact with his dazzling blue eyes.

"I'm a defense lawyer." He shrugs. "Leaves little time for a social life."

"Oh wow, that's fancy. I get the whole social life thing. I'm usually knee deep in the alphabet."

His easy-going chuckle settles a bit of my nerves but I can't erase the image of this handsome cat being ditched at the altar.

Scout and Taylor fight over what radio station to listen to and then move onto what restaurant we are going to eat at. Apparently Scout wants Italian and Taylor Mexican; with their raised voices it's hard to ignore.

"Is this what the couple life is?" I ask Connor, turning to him with a goofy smile.

"I guess."

I'm grateful when Connor goes on about his job and the different trials he's been involved in. He's only on his third one and seems a bit intense.

"I just get to deal with boogers and tears on my end."

"Yeah, but when they grow up, I'll be the one's defending their asses."

"Hey, they're not all bad."

"No, I agree." He turns to me, reaching for my hand. "But some are job security for me."

I force myself not to flinch when he clutches my hand. His palm is clammy and it feels awkwardly weird and a bit aggressive to be clutching onto me so soon. I try to determine if I can muster up a sneeze or a cough to get my hand back. But my luck, I'd probably pull a duo and fart at the same time.

"We're here," Scout chimes proudly from the front seat. "The best pasta in town."

"Guess we know who wears the pants in this relationship." Connor laughs at his own joke, but Taylor is quick to retaliate.

"I'm a smart man. I make her happy and I get puss later on tonight."

I cringe at the vulgarity of it. It's different when it's Scout and I bantering back and forth but when he's in the mix, it's just weird. But it's comments like those that my horndog best friend loves and thrives on.

"You bet you will, cowboy." She saddles right up to him, patting his chest. It's like he's her dog and sex is the proverbial bone.

Connor once again grabs my hand as we walk in. I'll give it to him, his hand grabbing game is on point. I can only focus on how odd and fishy his hand feels in mine. Scout is quick on shooting me a wink and waggling her eyebrows when she spots our two connected hands, but I just feel like a little school girl who is in trouble and being led down to the principal's office for a spanking.

We're seated at a cozy corner booth. Keyword cozy because there's no way to wiggle over to my personal bubble. Connor is on me like glue and after we place our order, he's practically dry humping my side. After continuous moments of him petting my hair and massaging my shoulder, I excuse myself to use the restroom.

Staring straight at my reflection in the mirror, I officially know this date is over and there will be no second date. I'm also chalking up the fact that blind dates will no longer ever happen in Olivia Olander's life. I'm calling my dad as soon as I get home and having him order me a mail order groom. I'll pick his looks and learn to live with him.

Quickly and with nimble fingers, I side braid my hair so Captain Grabby Hands can no longer molest my hair and then add a light layer of lip gloss to make me feel pretty. My heart stings a bit because Connor is gorgeous, just too damn quick on the trigger. *Maybe there's more to the story of his fiancé leaving him?*

I'll solve worldly problems another night because right now I have to stomach my way through this date. Connor is beaming up at me, patting my seat next to him when I get back. Our piping plates of pasta are laid out on the table. Scout is already in the process of making love to hers and from her erotic moans, I'd bet she's having an O right now before Taylor even gets his hands on her.

"More wine?" Connor smiles, filling my wine glass up for the third time tonight. Thank God that he's so creepy and has kept my impending buzz from impairing my judgment.

"I'll just have water, thanks." I try to wave him off but he just keeps on a pouring.

Swirling a massive forkful of angel hair pasta covered in a creamy alfredo garlic sauce, I stuff it in my mouth and then feel his lips press to my temple. The action, more abrasive than I expected, causes me to inhale the damn bit down my windpipe. The pasta leaves burns behind my throat as I try to choke it down.

I place the white cloth napkin in front of my mouth to mask the coughs and coax the pasta to go down. My stomach cramps up, knowing it should expel whatever has me choking so badly.

I hear Scout's voice. "She'll never be a swallower that girl, but seriously lay off Connor. I think you're making her uncomfortable."

And now I wish I was dead and six feet under. My best friend sticking up for me because I'm too big of wuss to do so. Connor nods and then I catch his gaze go to the other side of the restaurant, where's it been most of the night. Maybe he's eyeing his next catch. I mean, Scout had said he'd been busy fucking the countryside.

Why can't I just let him give me my first O and then shut the door on the topic? I know why; because I believe in love and see it on my parents' mantle in their wedding picture every time I'm at their house. My dad beaming proud and my mom with big doey eyes that look like she's afraid for her life. They grew together, the pictures morphed into happiness, love and joy. That's what I want and there lies the whole problem, because I live in a pit stop of a fuck and go society.

Connor finishes his meal quickly, still eying the table and miraculously my appetite has disappeared so I make different alphabet combinations with my noodles, dragging my fork slowly through the bowl.

And then like a deadly snake seeking its prey, Connor's arm is right back around my shoulder and then it all happens so fast. I hear Scout begin to scold him when I turn to Connor to ask him to remove his arm because he's making me extremely uncomfortable.

But when I turn to him, he seals his lips to mine and begins hoovering the shit out of my lips. The man has more suction than a vacuum.

"You bastard."

And it's like magic when the new voice joins us because his lip suction vanishes.

"Reba, nice to see you here," he says in a cheery voice.

"Found another whore, I see?"

The beautiful blonde with legs for days plants her hands on her hips.

"Have you fucked her best friend yet?"

"Oh Reba, still digging up bones are we? Guess you're beginning to miss what you left on your wedding day."

My head swivels back and forth between the two, aligning all the puzzle pieces. It's his ex-fiancé and that's why he'd been eyeing that table all night and more than likely a bit too grabby for my taste. I was the asshole's pawn.

"Well, payback is a bitch. I fucked your best friend, Scott, last week. His new nickname is Seis because I had six orgasms in sixty minutes."

Their war is clear as day, but what's a muffle is Scout shouting in the background for them to knock it off. At one point, she's pawing her way across the table towards the blonde before Taylor drags her back. Her right tit slipped from her extreme V-neck, dipping into her spaghetti sauce.

This has to be one very deranged and fucked up dream right now.

"Your Aunt Georgia was a better lay than you Reba, so carry on."

I look down to my plate of pasta, lost in a hopeless situation and stare at the "ch" digraph I drew with my fork. It's the next lesson for my first graders. The letters soon become a blur when Reba picks up the bowl of pasta, hoists behind her shoulder, and aims for Connor. And being the gentlemen he is, he swiftly ducks behind me, using me as his shield against the bowl of fucking pasta.

The letters c and h are now scattered all over my face, hair, and chest. Drops of pasta sauce and noodles snake down my cleavage and eventually drippings even cover my pretty pink toes.

"Fuck you and your pathetic life, Connor." From the sounds of heels clicking, Reba parades off.

I try to wipe the sauce from my eyes without getting it directly onto my pupil. Scout is attacking Connor as wait staff bring over mounds of cloth napkins.

"Stop," I sputter out with noodles dangling from my lips. "Just fucking stop."

I stand to my feet and realize I'm going to have to fucking skate out on my wedges under the sauce.

"This date is over."

"Olivia, sit down. We will take you home," Scout protests.

I count to ten in English, Spanish, and German to calm down before speaking and raising both of my hands.

"Goodnight. I'll catch an Uber home." I gracefully glide my wedge across the floor in a skating action because if I take a step, I'll eat shit. "Oh and Connor, you seem like a great guy, but get some damn counseling before you and Reba kill each other."

I silently thank my mother for enrolling me in ice-skating when I was five because I glide out of that Italian restaurant like a mother-trucking gold medalist. I shred the lace blouse and toss it in the nearest trashcan. But before I toss it, I use it to wipe down my limbs and face. It makes me sad to leave it behind since it was one of the sexiest things I had owned. It just bit the dust in the name of angry lovers.

I'm left in saucy skinny jeans and a tank top with nipples standing to attention in the night air. I perform a skating, walking duo combination that would even make Michelle Kwan proud to get at least a block away from the restaurant and then decide walking four more down to the center of town, knowing more Ubers will be available there. Knowing Scout, she'll beat Connor's ass and then come save me, but I just want to be left alone.

I pull my cellphone from my bag and notice the lit up red battery light with the notification of four percent battery life. Well, fuck me running into next Tuesday. I tap the Uber app as fast as possible and wait for it to connect me to a driver. A sigh of relief escapes when it shows at least ten cars surrounding me and only blocks away. I tap the green request button and everything goes black. My phone dies and I go bat shit crazy for a moment.

"You rotten damn asshole." I throw the phone without thinking into a brick building and watch it shatter into several tiny pieces into a bush. And if that's not good enough, I begin beating the shit out of the bush with my purse. Using it like an ax and mutilating it to shreds or at least that's what I feel like I'm doing. And if there were any homeless bums or bystanders standing on the lit up sidewalk, they've vanished.

A quick burst of red and blue lights light up the bush I'm currently going to town on and I freeze.

"Ma'am, are you okay?"

I'd recognize that rich sexy voice anywhere and now I want to jump into the fucking bush.

I pivot slowly, albeit a bit sexy, to cover up; shit, at this point I have no idea what I'm covering up.

"Hi." I wave and smile at Officer Oren.

"Olivia, is that you?"

I nod sheepishly while studying my alfredo covered toenails.

"Are you sure you're okay?" His voice is full of genuine concern.

"I'm fine, really; thanks for checking though." I send a chunk of my matted hair over my shoulder and hear some of the sauce splatter on the ground.

He holds both hands up in surrender. "Now, I'm not judging here or anything, but you were just karate chopping the shit out of that bush with your purse."

My shoulders slump down and I finally give in. "Blind date gone horribly wrong and my phone just died and I lost my lid."

"Are you carrying any weapons?" he asks next.

I shake my head side to side. "Just my purse."

"Okay then, I'll approach." He still has his hands up in the air but now a sexy smile spreads across his face.

I can't help but giggle.

"I must have looked pretty crazy, eh?"

He's only a foot from me and I can smell his musky cologne. "I almost called back up. I'm not going to lie."

This statement causes a full out belly laugh.

"And this?" he asks plucking a noodle from my shoulder.

I go to open my mouth, but he stops me before I can explain.

"But wait, if it's a crime you probably shouldn't tell me."

"Funny." I playfully whack his shoulder and damn, it's nothing but hard muscle. "You wouldn't believe it anyway."

"Try me." I watch as he bends over, collecting the contents from my purse scattered on the sidewalk. When he leans over the bush, I can't help but stare at his tight ass as it flexes when he moves.

"Are you staring at my ass?" His voice streams through the bushes.

I choke on my own spit.

"I'm just fooling with you, Olivia." He stands up with a handful of items, one being my cellphone or what is left of it. "You weren't joking when you said it was dead."

"I may have murdered it."

"I'll take you home. Get in."

"Do I have to ride in the back seat or get cuffed?"

"Do you want to be cuffed?" He raises an eyebrow at me and I feel the alfredo sauce heat up on my skin.

Instead of answering him, I crawl in the front seat, being careful not to smear my dinner on his leather seat. The smell of Oren is so strong in the cab I nearly weep.

HJ Bellus

Chapter 5

Saved By Mr. Lady Boner

"So she threw a bowl of pasta at Connor and him being such a man, hid behind me hence why I'm a walking, talking Italian dish right now."

"I shouldn't be laughing, but I can't believe this really happened." He smiles as he says it.

"No, you're going to go to hell laughing at a loser like me."

"You're not a loser, Olivia, I've seen you in action. Your students adore you and that Connor is a fool."

"It's not the first time," I admit.

"That you've had pasta thrown at you?"

"No," I swat his arm. "I'm not that big of a psycho. I mean a bad date. Actually, I've never had a good one."

"I'm sure your exes would say different."

"There are no exes."

He's stopped at a red light, and looks over to me. "Well then, the world is missing out Olivia Olander. I've only been around you a few times and can tell you're a great person."

The radio of his car interrupts us. I can't believe how easy it is to talk to him. I should be mortified with the state I'm in and to be sitting in his car. His voice is hypnotizing as I listen to him report back to the station about his night.

"It's been pretty quiet. Two speeding tickets and one domestic call. Oh, and I just nabbed the bush beating bandit of the county."

My eyes instantly grow to the size of golf balls and I send another punch to his arm. He clicks his radio back on the stand.

"Damn, I'm going to have to charge you for battery against an officer too."

I stop the question before it spills out of me, making the situation incredibly uncomfortable, but I want to ask if that would require cuffing.

"I'm so embarrassed." I cover my face.

"Don't be, Olivia, if you only knew some of the things I see on my shifts." He pauses to sniff the air. "But you are making me hungry."

My insides melt and pool together. I'd let Officer Sexy eat me anywhere and anytime. It's like he's reading the crimson flush racing across my face and my thoughts.

"I mean, your sauce is making me hungry." He slams his steering wheel with one hand. "Shit, that sounded even worse."

I can't help but laugh at the whole damn situation. "Yes, I'm hungry too."

"Dinner?" he asks.

"But you're working."

"If I get a call, then we'll have to go."

"My sauce." I point to my clothes.

"It's sexy and Italian is my favorite."

He exits the car and thankfully doesn't notice me turn the color of a purple beet from his compliment. *He's just a nice guy, Olivia.* For shit sakes, he's a community figure just doing his job with possibly a side of flirt.

I jump from the car before he has the chance to open my door.

"This has been my favorite diner since I was a young girl," I squeal under the bright red lights of Gravy Doug's.

"You've been here?" Oren asks in a shocked voice.

"Yeah, been coming here since well, I was in my mother's womb." I pause. "Well, that was awkward. But seriously, best place in town."

"I agree. I love hometown diners like this one."

"Oh my God, Oren, a chicken fried steak smothered in brown gravy right now sounds sooo good."

He grabs the old metal door handle to the diner and before he opens it, he says, "It's nice to see you smile, Olivia."

The asshole has manners to boot; using compliments combined with his killer looks, I'll never be able to look at another man the same. I wish he'd just morph into a captain dickhead right now so my wild imagination of me riding off into the sunset with him would diminish.

"Miss Olivia, we haven't seen you forever." Dolores, my favorite waitress, scurries over to me, giving me a one-arm hug while balancing a coffee pot in the other.

"Yeah, sorry; spring is hard, wrapping up the school year."

"How's your father?"

"Super busy and loving it."

"Good to hear, dear. Pick a booth and I'll be right over."

"Thanks, D."

I take a couple of steps from our one arm hug and hear Dolores greet Oren and tell him to sit wherever and instead of being an ass and embarrassing her, he just nods.

I sit in the booth and decide to spill it. "I've never had a boyfriend, I'm a bit awkward, loyal, own a dog named Pedro, and was raised by my dad since the age of nine."

The last part nearly rolls off my tongue, but I bite the end of it before I do and taste a smear of blood in my mouth.

"I like it." He nods, crossing his fingers on the table.

"You like it?" I ask.

"Yeah, I do. It's simple and honest."

"I guess." I push the menu to the edge of the table.

He relaxes back, stretching his arms on the back of the booth. I feel his legs sweep by mine under the table. "What should I order, Miss Olander?"

I blush when he calls me by my last name. "Um, you should get the homemade finger steaks, so I can steal one off your plate and dip it in my gravy."

"So you want to steal one of my sticks and dip it in your gravy?"

"Ass." I giggle and burry my face in my hands.

"I'm sorry. It's too easy to get you, Olivia."

"Tell Dolores I want the norm. I'm going to go scrape some of this shit off of me."

"Deal." He winks as I slide out of the booth.

When I look into the bathroom mirror, I wince in horror and disbelief. I really look like a walking plate of pasta. The brown paper towels in the bathroom are comparable to thirty-six grit sandpaper, but after soaked in warm water, do the trick of wiping away the mess from my skin. I don't even try to wipe the shit away from my jeans. My tank is mostly clean of debris and then to my hair. I finger comb the dried up sauce and noodles out the best I can, then add some water to my locks and wring it out with a paper towel. It's better than it was, but still not pretty.

"Dolores said you drink Diet Mountain Dew, so that's what I ordered."

"Perfect." I smile back to Oren. "What do you think of my Extreme Pasta Make-Over?"

I do a twirl before I sit down.

"I do like to eat so I'm a bit sad all the morsels are gone." He smiles, never breaking his stare.

"What a night!" My elbows plant onto the tabletop and I rest my chin in my cupped hands.

"You are gorgeous, Olivia, and I'm going to leave it at that because I'm on shift right now."

"Could I use your phone?" I ignore his compliment on the outside, but on the inside I melt a bit more.

Oren doesn't hesitate as he reaches down into his belt and holds out his phone.

"It's my personal, so feel free."

"Just going to text Scout, you know, the ladyboner gal in my room."

Oren only nods as he sips his black coffee.

"She's my best friend and Mr. Perfection Pasta was her boyfriend's cousin."

"Sisterwives?" he asks.

I stick my tongue out at him as my fingers race across the screen. I keep the message simple and tell her not to reply to this number and that I'll call when I get home.

I chew the rest of my meal in silence and just enjoy the eye candy before me and like a perfect prince, he lets me dip his stick in my gravy with no question.

His phone chimes halfway through our meal. "I think this is for you."

He hands me the phone after he's read the message.

Unknown: OMG Are you getting it on with someone? Just don't let a homeless bum steal your V card, O.

"Did you happen to read this?" I ask, peeking up at him through my fingers.

"Want me to lie?" he asks smiling a little bit.

I nod yes.

"Then no, I didn't see it." Oren shoots me a wicked grin.

"I'm going to stab her with a dull knife," I say, feeling the heat in my cheeks reach an all time high.

"I'll pretend that I didn't just hear your premeditated crime, Olivia."

"Right, Officer." I wink at him.

It's practically Chinese torture when I give Oren my address. He pays the bill like any gentleman, never trying to flirt again as he drives me home.

When we near my townhouse parking lot, I steady my legs for him to kick my ass out of his car, but he remains silent and very heroic.

"Thank you, Oren." I turn to him with honesty and my complete soul exposed to him. I feel his fingers wrap around my hand and it's a feeling I'm not use to. It's completely foreign and I'm not sure how to react, but it's warm and inviting, unlike the fishy experience earlier tonight.

"Olivia, I'd do and say so much more if I was off shift." His eyes beam in the moonlight.

I offer up a weak smile and let as many words flow as possible before melting down. "It's fine."

The harsh metal of the door slams shut and I walk my way up to my apartment in the lonely night. It's not until Pedro bounces up and down like a rabid rabbit that I finally exhale. It's a Friday night for the record books of epic proportion. I fall to my bed and let Pedro lick me clean of Alfredo sauce.

I dial Scout's number and the bitch doesn't even wait for a hello!

"Bitch, spill, now!"

"Scout, thank you so much for setting me up with Connor because this has been the best night of my life."

"Uh?" I hear my best friend's voice.

"I just experienced the best night of my life covered in sauce."

"Is this Olivia or a crack whore who beat her in the alley way for her phone? Either way, I'm cool. Oh wait, you're on your home line."

"It's O. I'm home next to Pedro and am on the mission for my O. You'll die when you hear the rest of the story."

I rattle on and on, spilling every single detail of the night until I hear Scout's light snores on the other end of the phone. Sleep never comes.

Dear Diary,

You wouldn't believe the shit that went down tonight. Pasta in the face and bush whacking on the blind date and it turned out to be the best night of my freakin' life. Officer Sex On A Stick saved the night and even took me to dinner at Gravy Doug's.

I love me some good gravy and then to top it off with a stiff fingersteak. TOUCHDOWN. More details to come soon, hopefully!

Love, O

Chapter 6

Let The Texting Begin

"Dad." The drilling noise and beating of metal continues. I scream a little louder this time. "DAD."

My father finally rounds the corner, wiping his brow with the handkerchief in his back pocket. He doesn't acknowledge me, but I know damn well he's heard me.

"Where's the parts order from this week?"

"Oh, I went to the local part store and I think the receipt is in the jockey box of my GMC."

"You think?" I ask, pissed off.

"I'm a mechanic and play in the grease."

"Well, keep your damn receipts you old fart. I'm a teacher, not a detective."

I typically look forward to my Saturdays at Dad's shop. I do his books for him, but this morning after a completely sleepless night, I feel like I'm losing my shit. Pedro's light snores from his dog bed underneath the desk don't help matters and only make me sleepier.

Dad's known as the best mechanic in town and is; however, his organizational skills lack. His office is always a mess with piles and piles of papers; some of it trash and others important documents.

I begin digging through the piles of papers, scouring for important receipts to update his monthly expense books, when my phone dings, alerting me to a text message. I'm sure sleeping beauty just woke up sated from amazing sex and is now ready for more details from my dinner with Oren.

An evil giggle escapes me as I punch in numbers into the computer program, aligning the expense with the check number written and imagine Scout throwing a hissy fit. When she's real determined, she'll start blowing my phone up and then she'll march her nosey ass right down here to the shop. I spilled all the details last night, but know she dozed off in the middle.

After a good hour of sorting and filing go by, I finally get to my new cellphone I picked up this morning on the way to dad's shop. One new text message lights up the home screen.

Unknown: Have any blind dates tonight that you need rescued from?

Me: ???

Unknown: I'm on night shift again and am willing to save you.

Me: Oren?

Unknown: Yep

Me: How?

Unknown: Your quite annoying friend

Me: But how?

Unknown: You texted her last night from my phone and then I did a little investigation of my own.

Me: Prove that it's you.

My heart races out of control, fingers tremble in excitement, and then I finally pinch myself to make sure this isn't another damn horny dream of mine.

"Ouch," I squeal after nearly ripping flesh from my arm and then my phone dings.

When I make eye contact with my phone laying on top of the desk, I moan. Yes, moan out loud in delight and mostly shock. Oren sent a picture alright and it just may be the sexiest picture I've ever seen.

It's him in what looks like a bathroom in boxers, bare chest, wet hair, and a dab of shaving cream on his chin. I pick up the phone, zooming in and out on all of his features. I don't miss the precious smirk dancing on his face in the picture. I take a moment to save his number and fight to muster up a coherent sentence to reply with.

Me: Well, hello Officer!

Oren: Your turn

Me: For?

Oren: A pic. I mean Scout could've given me the wrong number.

Me: No. Hell No.

Oren: Lol. Sorry, getting ready for work hence the bathroom pic

Me: Oh, don't be sorry

Oren: It would be nice to have a pic of you for my contacts.

Me: Persistent

Oren: Throw a dog a bone.

Scout is the selfie-whore. I only get in one when she's aiming the camera at the both of us. So, I fluff my messy bun, adjust my black nerd glasses on my face, slap my cheeks trying to put some color into them and try to take a few. FAIL.

I'm slapping the underside of my chin while testing all angles and even trying out duck lips when my dad walks in.

"Have you gone mad?"

Oh, that causes me to blush perfectly, throw my chin down, and snap a pic. And amazingly enough it turns out the best.

"It's for school, Pops."

"Interesting." He smiles back at me without saying a word before grabbing his phone and walking back out of his office.

Me: Here you go. I don't do selfies or send pictures, so consider yourself lucky!

In a not so patient manner, I tap the desk with my nails, staring at the phone screen, waiting on his reply. And then I see it or should I say, them. My boobies in all their glory overflowing from the top of my tank top give a whole new meaning to cleavage. *Holy shit, is that the top of my areola?* I was so damn worried about the angle of my face I didn't even notice the girls and their high beam headlights fully on display.

My phone dings once again in the small office and my butthole puckers out of fear.

"No, no, no."

"No, what?" I look up to Scout holding greasy take-out bags. "O, you're white as a ghost."

"I just sent a picture of my tits to Oren on accident."

"That's no assident." She giggles. Scout never misses a chance to pronounce accident the wrong way.

I shove my phone up into her face and cover my eyes. "Here, look."

She's only silent for a few seconds before she bursts out in hysterics. "O, you gave him a serious gun show, but looks like he liked it."

"Why?"

"He sent back heart emoticon smiling faces and then said *gorgeous* followed by the tongue with drool coming off of it."

"Oh shit." I slap my hands over my mouth.

"He likes you, O." Scout begins taking out the food and making everyone's plates. It's her official Saturday job. She knows Dad's favorites and spoils him.

I delicately pick back up my cellphone like there's a ticking time bomb in it and look at his reply. It feels good talking to him and I'm not ready to stop.

Me: Thanks

Oren: Text me tonight if you get trapped on another date from hell. I'm seriously worried about the health of the bushes in the community.

Me: Very Funny!!! But I'm done dating

Oren: Forever?

Me: I think it's best for society

Oren: Damn, I don't get a day off until next Friday and thought...

Me: By all means finish your thought

Oren: I'd like to have dinner with you since you've quit dating

Me: Deal

Shit, that was a bit aggressive and needy.

Oren: Have to head into work, but if you ever need anything please call this number.
Me: Thanks

"What's that shit-eating grin for?" Dad takes a seat in his favorite worn out black office chair, kicking back his heels, and digging into his food.

"Nothing," I grit out between my teeth and send Scout a death glare that could kill.

"You never told me how your blind date went, firecracker," Dad throws out between bites of his spicy chicken sandwich.

I'm not sure how to play this one out. If I tell my dad the real story of the pasta and how big of a doucher Connor was, he'd be out of the shop with his shotgun on the hunt. And if I tell him about my hopes with Oren he'll become overly excited.

I shrug. "It was fine."

Dad sputters on his chicken sandwich, flinging his legs down to the floor, and slamming on his chest. "I'm impressed."

"Well, it's complicated, Pops, so don't be going and getting your panties wadded up."

"I'm happy for you, Olivia, I really am."

I skip my chicken strips and tots and fill up my appetite with the picture of Oren on my screen. I save it, add it to his contact info, and then in a very tacky and desperate move, set it as my home screen. I move the apps around on the screen, so his broad chest and handsome face fill the screen and then let out a sigh.

"What's so interesting on your phone, firecracker?" My dad places his hand on my shoulder, trying to peek over at my screen.

"Nothing." I hit the sleep button. "Just looking up math lessons for Monday."

Pedro joins the conversation, jumping up and down barking for food. Scout gets my attention and she's suggestively pushing her tongue on the inside of her cheek and using a hand to make a crude motion.

"I'm off to work, girls behave."

She promptly quits her vulgar action as soon as he turns around.

"Now spill," Scout says as soon as Dad shuts the door.

"I did last night, bitch, you fell asleep."

"I didn't fall asleep. You make it sound so bad. I was sucked into a sex induced coma."

It doesn't take much convincing to retell the whole tale to her. Halfway through the story I realize for the first time ever, I'm actually happy and hopeful.

Chapter 7

Meet Tony the Tiger

"So, when is the big field trip?" Scout asks, while shoving half a banana in her mouth. I can't even begin to imagine how much dick she's used to housing in there.

"Earth to O. I asked you a question."

"Thursday."

"Are you excited? Think you'll see him?"

I just shrug and pick through my dismal salad.

"What's wrong, Champ?" She nudges me in the shoulder.

"I seriously have no business messaging Oren and letting him take me out on a date or I mean, dinner?"

"Why?"

"Because I have no friggin' clue what I'm doing? Hell, I've never even been kissed before, Scout."

"Here."

I watch Scout scoot her chair closer to mine, then wipe off her lips with the back of her hand and before I know what in the hell is happening, she has her lips sealed to mine.

"Scout." I push her back and scrub the shit out of my lips with my napkin.

"See, now you have nothing to worry about." She points over her shoulder. "And we just gave every veteran male teacher in this staff lounge a boner."

"God, how have I stayed friends with you this long?"

She slaps both the tops of my thighs. "Seriously, O, I've given you the most powerful vibrator on the market along with a clit stimulator and have told you to watch porn. I mean, you need to get a little loosened up if hot cop is going to turn into something real."

"I can't, Scout."

"Just go home tonight, run yourself a nice hot bubble bath, pour you some wine, set the mood music, and then let Tony the Tiger sneaks his way in."

"Just stick it in my vagina?"

Did those words just really come out of my mouth in the teacher's staff lounge?

"Like I said, you need to get lose, strum your clit-tar to get revved up, and then sink it in."

"No, I'm so done with this conversation." I slam my lunch box shut and feel more hopeless than ever. I'm really starting to believe that some women are just destined to be alone forever. It's all too overwhelming to think about.

I make my way down to my classroom, high fiving each of my friends and then save the day teaching one math problem after another. My mind fights me on every single step though. I'm constantly checking my phone for a text from Oren. He's been texting randomly and I can't get enough of it.

When the bell rings and I usher the students out, I only stay until contract time instead of six or seven at night grading papers and prepping tomorrow's lessons.

"I can't believe I'm going to do this," I say to my reflection in my rearview mirror. "I'm not even a wine drinker for Christ's sake."

On nervous high heels, I walk into the store, toss in my normal items and then hit the wine aisle. My sweaty palms run over the front of my tight khakis as I look at all the wine. *Holy shit, it's like the mecca of wine here.* Reds, whites, pinks, some in boxes, others in fancy glass bottles and not one even speaks to me, so I pull out my phone and Google the best wine for a newbie. Google recommends Moscato and I go for it, throwing in the biggest bottle I can find on the shelf.

This is going to take massive amounts of courage if I even do it. After school, Scout reassured me that Tony the Tiger is waterproof and will for sure give me an O. I'd like for my first O to be from a real body part, not a synthetic gigantic impression of a cock that can glide, twirl, and vibrate. My phone dings while I wait in line.

Oren: Hello Miss Olander.

Me: Good day Hot Cop

We've both become a little more unguarded over our few days of texting.

Oren: Only a few more nights until we dine together.

Me: I won't lie. I can't wait and it's two nights.

Oren: I was thinking of taking you out for pasta

Me: Lmao. Of course you were. Hey, I'm checking out and will text when I get home.

At least the man has jokes, so far never making anything awkward. My skin crawls when the cashier scans the wine and then takes her time tucking it in a brown paper bag. I swear she knows that I'm going home, slugging back some wine, and then getting it on with huge plastic dick. I've never slid my card so fast through the reader and punched in my pin.

"Fancy seeing you here."

A quick flash of red and blue lights grabs my attention and then my gaze lands on Oren in his patrol car with his arm resting out the window. He slowly pulls his sunglasses up to the top of his head and smiles sweetly at me. Oh, those dark brown eyes and strong jawline will be the death of me.

"Are you following me?"

"Maybe." He shrugs. "It's not illegal to be attracted to a gorgeous woman."

"No, but it is illegal to be that cheesy."

We both share a good laugh and I step closer so I can get a whiff of his cologne. I melt when it hits me.

"Have a hard day at work?" he asks, pointing to the neck of the wine bottle peeking out from the bag.

I go speechless with no witty answer. It takes me moments to recuperate. "It's for a friend."

"That's what all the good girls say, Olivia."

He drives alongside me slowly until I reach my car and pop the back hatch with my remote. I turn to him after I settle my bags in and place both hands on my hips.

"Need something, Officer?"

He uses his pointer finger, beckoning me to come closer. I close the space and bend down a bit. Oren snakes his arm around the back of my neck, tugging me closer into him, his large palms splayed out on the back of my neck, and then whispers in my ear.

"Your ass looks killer good in those pants. Wear them Friday." He keeps our closeness for a second before dragging his lips along the lower lobe of my ear before backing all the way back.

"And Miss Olivia Olander this is why I can't be around you when I'm on shift," he says with a smile. "The bad guys would be torching the city while I'm all wrapped up in you."

A call comes across his radio and he does his best to pay attention and then gives me a wave as his sirens and lights go on. The shrill sound of the sirens sends goose bumps racing up and down my spine.

I plop down in the driver's seat of the car with my knees still knocking together from the contact and his words. I send him a text that I know he won't see for several hours, since he just raced off in such a hurry.

Me: I can't wait for the handcuffs.

And from there on it's radio silence, which means those red and blue lights mean serious business. I drive home in the safest mid-size SUV thanks to my pops and look over at my bottle of wine every once in awhile. When I hit my front door, the bottle of wine practically shouts my name from the brown paper bag. I swear the fucker is screaming my name and taunting me the whole time to get my O on.

Pedro does hot laps around me, bounding all over the apartment, only holding still for a couple of pets and then doing more hot laps. I swear my neighbor slips him crack while I'm away at school.

"Walk." I hold up his harness and smile when he slides between my feet. He loves going on walks and it's rare in the springtime considering how late I typically get home. Wrapping up the school year is always hell.

Fresh air will do my mind good right now, like get me in game mood for the main event later in the bathtub. Pedro sits perfectly letting me snap his harness on. Boy, that took us a good year to get down; it used to be like a damn WWE wrestling match with dog hair flying and me cussing.

Once it's snapped, he paws me with his paw, kindly reminding me to feed him his Pupperoni for being a good boy.

"You are so spoiled, little boy." I ruffle the top of his head and toss him his snack. "I love you."

I scoop Pedro up, letting him eat the rest of his treat and jog down my stairs with my cute little doo-doo bag in my other hand. The sun is bright and I curse myself for forgetting my shades, but know this will be a short walk today since my mind is seriously preoccupied.

Pedro takes off on a run down the sidewalk, using all of his leash and even tugging on my hand more. Yep, someone has to be slipping him crack. I look down at my tight khakis and giggle, remembering the compliment Oren gave me. The flip-flops I slipped into before leaving slap the sidewalk rhythmically and my thoughts float away to hot cop. His scent, smile, and voice; it all has me locked in a trance.

"Time to turn around, Pedro."

We reach the end of our block and I don't feel like crossing the main road tonight. Pedro does some dirty business on a patch of grass and like any other responsible dog momma, I scoop it up.

A flood of sirens assault me when I stand back up. At least a dozen cop cars whiz by us with their lights and sirens blaring. Something big must be going down right now. They go by too fast to even be able to recognize Oren. I try to shrug it off and head back where my wine awaits my company.

The walk seems to have worn out Pedro. He lays perched at the bottom of my bed soaking up the little bit of sunlight streaming through the window. I forgo eating due to nerves and pour a glass of wine after nearly elbow dropping the top of the bottle to get the cork out. Who knew a simple machine was so damn difficult to use?

At first the tartness of the wine makes me shiver but then soon, a sweet spray dances over my tongue.

"Not bad," I say to myself and down the glass.

The stage is set. A hot bubble bath, a full wine glass, bottle of wine, light mood music, candles, and then...the massive purple plastic cock who is about to give me my first screaming O. I locked Pedro in his kennel because there's no way I could handle him watching me rub this one out or at least try to.

The water stings my skin as I sink down into the tub. My favorite sweet scent of bubble bath assaults my senses as I melt back into the tub. I sip down another glass of wine, relaxing even more with Norah Jones singing in the background. I was smart enough to keep the bottle in reaching distance for refills.

My fingers can barely wrap around the girth of the vibrator. How in the hell is it supposed to fit inside me? I giggle to myself when I realize I'm holding the damn thing like a microphone near the tip of it.

"Welcome ladies and gentlemen to the virgin diaries starring Olivia Olander who's currently O-less and in desperate search for *The Big O.*"

I belly laugh like a crazed idiot after my entertaining stance. I down one more glass of wine and then dial up Scout for one last burst of encouragement.

"Scout," I purr into the phone.

"Sup, ho-bag?"

"Just floating in the tub, slamming wine, and about to get it on with Tony the Tiger."

She squeals a tone deafening pitch into the phone before creating any coherent speech. "I'm so proud of you, O. Just make sure to get used to the vibrating speeds before full insertion and once in, set the twirl mode to level three and you'll be flying high."

I feel like I should be taking notes instead of nodding and sipping my adult grape juice. The influences of the wine have me fully accepting her advice instead of flushing with embarrassment and running away.

"I think I got this, Scout."

"Get it, girl." She laughs into the phone. "How much wine have you pounded?"

"Like only half a bottle, but it's one of those jumbo ones."

"You do realize that's like three bottles in one, right?"

"Is that bad?" I belch before getting out the last word.

"Don't drink anymore and just get down and dirty."

A beep sounds on my phone. I pull it away to look at the screen. "Gotta go, Scout, Hot Cop is calling me."

"O don't you dare take it."

"Bye." I click over to the next call, giddy as a little kid in a candy shop.

"Hello." I try to purr in my sexiest of sexy voices.

"Hey Olivia." His rich voice sends shivers down my spine and I swear they land right between my legs. I tingle.

"Everything okay? I swear there were cop carzz everywhere."

Shit, did I just slur one of my words into the phone? I sit up a bit taller in the water and try to pay attention. The cool air perks my nipples right up.

"All is good, Olivia. There were two different things going down, that's why there were so many cars everywhere." He pauses and I hear the cracking slam of a few doors shutting.

"What are you doing?" I ask out of curiosity.

"Just got home and ready to crash, but felt bad the way I left you today."

"I get it. It's your job. No worries. I'm not a needy person, Oren."

"Just trying to be a gentleman to my new non-dating friend." His voice muffles for a second and then becomes clearer.

"What are you doing now?" I ask.

"Just took my shirt off, getting ready to kick my boots off, and drink a brewski before hitting the hay."

"So you're topless?" My nipples stiffen instantly picturing Oren shirtless.

"Yeah." He chuckles. "You interested?"

"Possibly."

Oh those tingles intensify to a mind numbing state. I can do this. I can really do this with Oren's voice fueling my desire.

"Picture?"

"Duh," I promptly reply.

"Give me a second. Oh, and Olivia, we still on for Friday?"

"Fucking A we are." I slap my hand over my mouth when the bold words fly out. *Note to self: less wine.*

His deep chuckle vibrates through the phone. "The answer I wanted."

"Before we say goodbye, give me a second."

"Okay, I need to whiz real quick."

Holy shit, he's about to be holding his big gigantor wiener in his hand. Baby Jesus, don't let him be packing light.

"Alrighty then, I'll be right back."

I set down my cell phone on the edge of the tub and stare down Tony. And then sing "Let's get it on" to him. It's the biggest move of my life and I'm about to become a full-fledged woman and if things do ever go further with Oren, I'll be ready.

His deep voice snaps me out of my hypnotic stare with Tony.

"I'm here," I holler. I down the remaining wine in my glass grab my phone and then Tony with the other hand. "Thanks for the call tonight, Officer Hot Cop."

I plunge Tony down into the water, fumbling for the buttons. His edges are a bit more rigid then I remember as I try to softly rub him up and down my clit. It's the first step to strum my clit-tar.

"Oren, you there?"

It's silent on his end; boy, he must have a huge bladder or maybe tired out from holding up his monster cock.

"Oren?" I try again while still strumming away and by the way, it's an awful feeling. Very abrasive indeed.

My phone begins to vibrate in my hand and then furiously twirls while vibrating. I pull my phone from my ear and come face to face with fucking Tony the Tiger. I was talking to a damn vibrator with the tip of the cock to my ear.

"Oh fuck," I squeal, pulling my phone from between my legs, soaked in my favorite scent of bubble bath and dripping water.

Chapter 8

Load That Bus, Kids

"Never again will I listen to you, Scout." I thump her in the chest with each word. "I could've died."

Scout doesn't seem affected by my pissed off mood or the fact of me dying by electrocuting my vagina.

"I told you not to answer the call, but no, love stricken O just couldn't listen."

"I'm not in love, asshole." I flop down in one of her student's chairs, kicking my legs up on a desk.

"Then what is it?"

I ignore her question. "God, can you imagine the headline? Ontario first grade teacher found dead in her tub with vibrator to her ear and pubes fried from her cellphone."

"Not gonna lie, it would've been epic shit," Scout replies, not missing a beat as she writes vocabulary words on her board.

"I hope I don't see him today."

"I'm sure he volunteered to lead the field trip just to see you."

"Whatever." I trace the cock and balls carved into one of the student's desks.

"He does." Scout pauses writing and swirls around to face me. "I know he does because I talked to him."

"You what?" My finger stops on the tip of the poorly drawn dick.

70

"He called and asked for you number." She holds up a hand. "And before you freak, he got my number from when you texted me."

"What did he ask you?"

"Well, for your number, and he hinted around about asking you out and oh yeah, your bra size."

"You're a dick, Scout."

"I'm only teasing about the bra size part, but seriously O, he's into you."

"I doubt that. He's just a nice guy."

The bell rings to kick off the morning, I stand from the chair, and stare down at my hot pink tennis shoes. I love field trips, hence the casual wear. Before I open the door to Scout's room, I holler over my shoulder, "You have quite the artist in your room. The desk I was sitting in has a nice picture of cock and balls engraved into it."

"Those little bastards," she mutters before I shut the door behind me.

Scout's room is in an outside modular since the fifth grade is the oldest grade in the school and our building has simply just run out of space. I envy her in having her own little island. She can open and close the windows in her room and always gets a shot of fresh air when she walks into the main building. I think I've officially diagnosed myself with spring freaking fever. I need May thirtieth to get here real soon.

It takes less than forty minutes to take roll, make sure each student uses the restroom, assign buddies for the field trip, and load the big yellow bus. The station is on the other side of town, so not a long ride, but way too far to trot little first graders over to it.

My nerves are at an all-time high with thoughts of seeing Oren. I haven't talked to him, well, since sinking my phone down yonder. This is the second phone in less than two weeks. I'm screwed and the even bigger question is what am I going to tell him happened? What if he thinks I'm mad at him? Or what if he can read minds and will be able to see the whole terrible scene playing out with me holding a big purple dick to my ear while trying to get off on my cellphone.

"Oish." I place the palm of my hand on my forehead.

"Forget something?" Kane asks, looking up at me.

"No." I try to search for an excuse, but give up. "Never mind."

It just so happens that Kane was magically partnered with me. I don't need him explaining his family's history at the station or karate chopping Nathaniel in the nuts while listening to a lecture. He keeps me on my damn toes that's for sure and has pushed every single button of mine, but there's something about him I adore. Steered in the right direction, the little sandy haired, toothy grinning critter will go far in life one day and I won't lie, that's a big if, but I love him.

I ruffle his out of control hair and tell him what I try to tell him everyday he enters my class. "You're a smart boy, Kane, and will go far."

I stand up and face the back of the bus. The station is only blocks away and my little gems can use all the reminding they can get.

"One, two, three, eyes on me." I clap five times and wait for their undivided attention. Oh, little first graders are such fined trained things in May. It makes my heart all gushy inside.

"Reminder, friends, we are going to be on our best behavior. Let me remind you what we brainstormed in class yesterday. We listen, raise our hands to talk, and keep our hands to ourselves." I grab the back of my seat as Jan the man, the bus driver, just flew over a speed bump at Mach speed.

"You almost ate shit," Kane says and then giggles.

I flash him a death glare and remind him. "Language, Kane."

While the whole time thinking, you little asshole.

"You'll earn tickets on this field trip for good behavior and also asking appropriate questions. Remember only ask questions, don't tell stories."

Jan aka bitchy bus driver slams on the breaks, throwing me forward into the back of the seat. One boob hikes up over the seat while the other is basically decapitated into the back of the seat. And Johnny and Mikey just smile at my one boob peeking up and out of my shirt.

"Remain seated until I stop," Jan growls.

I stand up, tamping down my anger and turn to her. "Ironic, you're stopped and I'm not standing."

My middle finger itches to send her the bird, but I just smile and cuss her out in my head because let's face it, she'd pound my face in in a fist fight. *Lovely way to start off the field trip.*

The students file off the bus successfully with no other incidents and we march right in to the front of the station and wait for the captain to join us. The station is buzzing with bodies moving about everywhere doing their jobs. I scan the room, looking for him. I want to tell him I broke my phone again or I guess at the very least, leave a note for him.

"Hi, I'm Captain Sorenson and you must be Miss Olander."

"Yes, I am." I extend my hand to shake his.

"Officer O'Brien had nothing but glowing remarks about you and your class."

I'm hoping he'll make me glow one day.

"He was great and the students loved him. They're very excited about this field trip today."

"Okay, we'd like to split them into three groups and rotate in stations so they get a more hands on experience."

"Perfect, I'll assign mothers with each group and then roam between."

It takes me no time to strategically organize the groups and send them on their way. I follow close behind Kane's group, but allow him some space as well. He's clearly intrigued by the tour of the office for now. Hopefully the field trip will hold his attention long enough before he resorts to any form of nut karate kicking.

"So, is this the bush beating bandit you apprehended the other night?"

I spin around on my heels when I hear his deep chuckle. Officer Sexy is leaned against a desk with feet crossed at the ankles and his arm over his chest. Another officer is perched in a chair behind the desk. He's opposite of Oren in an older, pudgy way.

I curl my lips in, trying to hide the smile wanting to dance across my face. Just seeing him makes me light up inside and outside. The man has my number.

"Olivia," he draws out in his deep voice.

"Officer." I nod back.

The man behind his desk stands up and tips his hat at me. "She's as beautiful as you described, Oren."

And then he limps off out of sight.

"That's Chuck."

My face is heated crimson red from embarrassment, allowing me only to nod.

"Sorry, he's my only bud since moving here."

"It's fine," I finally squeak out.

"You haven't texted me and your phone goes straight to voicemail."

"About that." I raise my finger and blush an even deeper red. "I uh- It fell in the tub."

Oren pushes up from the desk, closing the space between us. "You were talking to me while in the tub."

I nod when I realize the rest of my body is paralyzed from his nearness and musky smell.

"Naked in the tub and talking to me." One of his dark eyebrows shoots up.

I can literally feel my V card burst inside me. I may have just had my first O the way my insides tingle and whirl around.

"I'm excited for our dinner." God, I sound like a fucking idiot.

"And again, Olivia, this is why I can't be around you when I'm on duty." He points down between us to his tented pants.

I gasp and then slap my palm over my mouth and then look into his eyes. *Could I seriously be anymore of a ten year-old little girl right now?*

"I have a tour of my cop car to give, Olivia."

"Then I have a tour to attend." I wink at him.

"God, I wish it was Friday, Sexy Teacher."

And I keep my eyes glued to his taut ass in his slacks as he saunters away from me.

"Headlights, Miss Olander." I pry my gaze away from the sexiest ass on the planet to see Kane with both of his pointer fingers sprung out from his chest and his little eyebrows waggling at high speed.

And as sure as shit, high beams are on full force. I need to get control of those damn things when around Oren.

"Oh Kane." I ruffle his hair and follow his small group around to the different stations. All the questions the students ask make me proud and it's one of the rare and genuine moments in teaching where I'm proud beyond words.

The little group I tag along with, which includes Kane, stops outside for their last station. Stepping out into the glaring sunlight, I pull down my Ray Bans and smile when I spot Oren.

I feel a little hand in mine and when I look down, it's Kane staring up at me, doing his best to shade his eyes with his hand. "Do you like him?"

"Uh?" I heard the question clear as day, but I think it's the shock coursing through my body that makes me speechless.

"Do you like Officer Lady Boner?"

"Kane." I squeal a bit too loud and cover my mouth.

"I heard Ms. Johnson call him that one day when I came back in for my homework."

"It's Officer O'Brien and he's a nice man."

"You want to make babies with him, uh?"

"Kane, where do you get this stuff from?"

"My sister in high school. She says that every time Channing Tatum comes on TV and then her friend tells her to quit dry humping her pillow."

"You need to not listen to your sister, but can I tell you a secret?"

Kane perches up on his toes and I lean over to whisper in his ear. "I do think he's kind of cute."

"Well, if you two decide to make babies together and he's mean to ya, I'll karate him in the nuts."

I clutch his little hand in mine and just shake my head while we make our way closer to the group gathering around the cop car. "Kane, do you know what it means when your sister says that?"

"Oh yeah."

I cringe and send up a Hail Mary. "What does it mean?"

"When you make your dog play Barbies."

I wait for his punch line or devilish grin, but he goes into a long-winded story about one time of a making baby session that involved a chichiwawa and a few Barbies. Sometimes I wonder what some of the moms smoked while preggo and definitely think his older sister needs a stern lesson in using the earmuffs tactic when around Kane.

"Okay, shhh, buddy, let's listen." I pat Kane's shoulders and square him up to Oren who's ready to begin.

Just like in the classroom, Oren entertains the kids, explaining and showing them the different parts to his car. And of course, even the curious boys start asking about pepper spray, guns, and if he's ever had to take someone down. Oren stuns me with how gracefully and comfortable he is with little kids. Most men his age tend to stove up and brush them off.

"Any other questions?" Oren asks, surveying our little crowd for a moment.

Kane turns around to me and whispers, "Want me to see if he has a chichiwawa?"

The giggle escapes before I can stifle it. "No, Kane. It's fine."

Amy in the front shoots her hand up and Oren calls on her, letting the class know it's the final question before it's time to head to the bus.

"Can you handcuff our teacher?"

It's the first time I see Oren flush with embarrassment and possibly the cutest thing I've ever witnessed.

"You'd like what?" He clears his throat.

"Can you put handcuffs on Miss Olander?"

He takes a moment to glance up at me before shaking his head from side to side. "Why would you want to see your teacher in cuffs?"

She only shrugs while the rest of the class starts chanting cuff her, cuff her. It takes Oren a moment to get his bearings before he holds up his hand to silence the class and then curls his pointer finger at me.

"Miss Olander, the students would like to see you in cuffs."

"Go." A choir of little voices shout and begin to tug me by my wrists.

I finally make my way through the group up to him and whisper in his ear while the students continue to cheer, "About time you cuff me."

"Olivia." He curls in his lips, stopping his words for a second. "You are going to be the damn death of me."

And I swear to the virginity gods all over the world that in this moment I have every ounce of courage to reach up on my tiptoes and kiss his plump sexy-ass lips, but then I'm reminded of where I am.

Oren spins me around so fast I can't even begin to comprehend what's going on. Dirty thoughts race in my mind, but I know none of that's about to go down.

"You always need to be swift, smart, and accurate in your decisions when apprehending someone." Oren tilts his face down towards the crook of my exposed neck, letting out a puff of air that tickles my tender skin.

"Friends, you're so silly for wanting to see me in cuffs," I say with a huge smile back to my students, trying to distract myself from the rock hard body pressed up to the back of mine.

Oren continues on. "Sometimes you just know deep down in your gut that you have the bad guy captured, but other times it takes more investigating and paperwork."

Click. Click. Click. The cold metal snaps around my wrists. Oren intertwines his fingers in mine, gently squeezing as he keeps on with his speech. I don't miss one of his hidden messages.

"There's times when you come across a person who fits the description perfectly and you have the worst time shaking it until you finally give in."

Amy shoots her hand up. "How does that have to do with anything?"

I whirl around, showing the students the cuffs and let them have fun squealing and clapping before Oren undoes the cuffs. I turn to him before ushering the students to the bus. Glancing down quickly, I spy his tented pants once again and can't help internally fist pump the air.

"Thanks, Oren."

"See you tomorrow, Olivia."

"You mean Miss Olander." We both look over to see Kane with a beaming smile.

"You're correct, sir. See you tomorrow, Miss Olander."

This time it's Kane who clutches to my hand. "You better pray that man has a chichiwawa, Miss Olander."

Chapter 9

The Humping Dog Syndrome

"Fuck, shit, bitch." I sling the foundation bottle across the bathroom.

"Calm yo' titties before you stroke the fuck out, O." Scout picks up the bottle. "I've brought all my stuff."

"Perfect because my olive colored skin will look perfect in fucking albino foundation."

"Saying fuck every other word is not going to help your case in getting sausage in your wound-up taco tonight."

"Scout." I glare at her.

"Sit." She pushes me down on my vanity stool. "You left a bottle at my house awhile back and I have it."

"Why am I so nervous? I don't date anymore; it's just dinner."

"It's a date and the first one you've ever been super excited about. I'll get you one glass of wine in a second. ONE glass, O."

"Yeah, I know. I came in like a seasoned veteran last time with the wine."

"I love you." Scout kisses my cheek before bouncing out of the bathroom.

I hear the racket of glasses and the fridge door slamming shut. I catch my reflection in the mirror and study it. *Why in the hell would a man like Oren be attracted to me?* Almond shaped eyes, rich olive toned skin, a boring face with proportional features, straight long black hair, and that lingering question of what ethnic groups came together to make a freak like me.

"Knock it off." Scout hands me the glass of wine. "I'll never understand why you can't see your beauty, O. Shit, more men wanted you in college."

"Whatever." I down half the glass.

"It's just my size D tits they're attracted to. They all eyed you for your looks, genuine personality and real size C girls."

"I don't know what it is." I shrug.

Scout busies herself applying my make-up and chattering away. "It's hard for you not having your mom growing up. Don't you remember us always in awe of her beauty and your dad smitten with her?"

"Yeah," I nod. "She was the most gorgeous woman I've ever seen."

Wine splatters on my forehead and the bridge of my nose as Scout's hand connects to the side of my face in a punishing slap.

"Then why can't you ever see yourself as her? Jesus, do you think you have your dad's nose that's the size of Texas and that wart on his jawline or his wiry gray hair?"

"Be nice," I say as I wipe off the speckles of wine.

"I am, but I refuse to let you beat yourself down and not love yourself, O. You're gorgeous. Oren sees that, so go have fun tonight."

"Okay, okay, Mom."

"Let him kiss you, finger you..."

"Shut the hell up, bitch."

Scout kneels down in front of me, wiping the rest of the wine from my face and fixing my makeup. "Seriously, and I know we aren't serious very often, but Olivia, I worry about you. You're too hard on yourself. You're a gorgeous, strong, stubborn, and very amazing person. You deserve a better half, so quit degrading yourself."

"Thanks, Scout."

She reaches up, seizing my nipple between her finger and thumb and gives it one hell of a twist. "Now, let's get you dressed up like a first rate hooker."

She bounds off into the other room before I can talk and I'm left staring into the mirror. For the first time, I see hints of my mom in my features. I'll never be as beautiful as her and never was meant to be. I'm the perfect combination of her and my father. I'll never admit it to Scout, but she's right.

I walk into my bedroom. "He told me to wear my tight khakis."

"Perfect! Pair it with this tight titty hugging peach lacy blouse and these heels."

"Heels? Um no, we are going to dinner, not the damn opera."

"You'll wear them and wow him."

"It's too much, Scout. I'll look desperate."

"What's the problem with that?" She rearranges her messy bun on the top of her head. "I'm pretty sure dragging your whole class down to the station screamed desperate."

"I guess you're right. I am desperate."

"Desperate to get Officer Sexy's ding dong in your pie hole."

"Oh my God, I can't even, Scout. What if he kisses me and I screw it up?"

"Oh honey, you will." She steps up to me, picking at the top I just threw on. "But it will be good memories to look back and laugh at just like your attempt at death by cellphone in kitty."

I flush with embarrassment just thinking about that. My new phone is on the way from the company and I received a very passive aggressive email about reaching my limit on my cellphone insurance.

"You'll never let me live that one down, will you, Scout?"

"Not looking good at all." She bounds out of the room leaving her voice streaming through the hall. "I have an idea."

"Shit." I cringe. "I'm done with your ideas, biotch."

I scoop up Pedro, who's curled in all the clothes thrown on my bed. "Your auntie is cray-cray and I swear, on a mission to kill me."

"Okay, this is our favorite site when we want to spice things up." Scout's perched on the couch with my personal MacBook in her lap.

"First, who is we and second, what are we spicing up?"

"Taylor and sometimes we play a game of watching steamy porn and see how long we can go with keeping our hands to ourselves."

84

I sneak another glass of wine, realizing I think I'm already a full-fledged wino. "I don't even want to know."

I'm pretty sure Scout ignores each word that leaves my mouth.

"I made it about three minutes one time until I couldn't resist Taylor anymore and sealed the deal with my lips around his..."

"Shut the hell up. I don't need the visual."

"O, here watch this." She stands and hands me my laptop. "It will help you loosen up and hey, look at it like you're doing homework. You need to be prepared."

"We are not humping tonight," I exclaim.

"Stranger things have happened." Scout waggles both of her eyebrows at me. She pretends to punt Pedro across the room before waving bye. "Make sure you watch that shit. It'll have you fucking like a porn star before you know it."

Pedro growls at Scout, hence the reason I know dogs can sense evil, when Scout slams the door. I sip the last of my allotted wine, not wanting to be trashed for my date. I set the laptop on the counter and it whisper screams my name, taunting me to take a peek. It's just like a bad accident you can't peel your eyes from. Damn curiosity has me all balled up in wonderment.

The wine glass clinks when I set it down on the counter and without another thought, I flip open the screen and wait for it to boot up. Skin, more like a sea of flesh, covers my entire screen. Ginormous peepees and women's voluptuous breasts dance in motion. And that's about all I can handle. My finger accidentally clicks on a link before I have a chance to boot down the laptop.

"Holy mother loving burning butthole." I squeal and slam my palm over my mouth as I watch a wanger slam into a butthole over and over again. Both of the moans and whimpers streaming from the video are very deep and masculine and then that's when I see a pair of hairy nuts dangling below the butthole.

"Holy shit!" I slam the screen shut. "I'm going to fucking kill Scout."

Besides scrubbing out my eyes with a wire brush and pounding in Scout's face, there's not much left to get that visual out of my head. I resort to falling back down on the couch and dialing up the one person who always gives me the confidence to push ahead in life. Good ol' Daddio.

"Hello." His asshole dog yaps in the background, making it hard to hear Dad's voice.

"Hey, Pops."

"Olivia, now aren't you glad I forced you to keep your landline?"

I roll my eyes and remember the fight we had over me getting a landline. "Yes, Pops, you were right."

"I just know how clumsy you are and I never want you without communication."

"Yeah, my new one is on the way, but my insurance cut me off."

"Too many claims?"

"Bingo."

"Well, just try to be careful, hun."

Oh, if I had a dollar for every time he's told me that, I'd have enough money to buy my first O.

"Yeah, yeah."

"So, what are you up to? Calling me on a Friday night and I don't hear Scout in the background."

"Well, Pops, I'm..."

I stall because the next few words are so damn foreign to me that I'm not sure that I even know how to begin to process them.

"Gay? Getting a sex change?"

"Dad," I squeal in between giggles. He always knows when a heavy topic is coming.

"I'm going on a date, Dad."

"Very good. Another set up disaster type?"

"No, remember the other day when I said the blind date went well but was complicated?"

"Yeah."

"Well, it's that guy. Oh, Jesus. I mean it's a guy I met that night."

"Very good, Olivia. You must like him if you're giving it a second chance."

"Honestly, Dad, I'm scared."

"That's a good feeling to have dear. I'll never forget how terrified I was when I flew over to meet your mother." He pauses and I know it's because he's getting choked up. He rarely talks about the whole process of him purchasing a mail order bride.

"It's okay, Dad."

"No, Olivia, listen to me. I wanted to fly home before I met her. I was sick thinking of all the bad things that could've gone wrong, but the second I laid eyes on her she made every single wrong in the world right in my eyes. And all my nerves vanished. I brought your mother home, married her, and then we finished off our fairytale with you."

"Ahhh, Dad, now you're going to make me cry and I'll tell Scout that you messed up my make-up."

"Shit, don't do that. I'm afraid of that girl."

I laugh into the phone, petting the top of Pedro's head. "I love you Dad, even if I inherited all your awkward genes."

"Olivia, you're the world to me and I want nothing more than for you to find that hopeless and endless love like I did with your mother."

A knock at the door distracts me, saving me from a full-blown fit of tears. "He's here, Pops, I gotta go. I love you so much."

"Update tomorrow at the shop."

"You got it. Bye."

He hangs up the phone in his typical abrupt fashion. The man never says good-bye. Refuses to say the word, claiming why say it when I'm not going anywhere.

With sweaty palms and all, I take each step to the door with a mixture of excitement and whole lot of nerves. Pedro yaps and barks like his ass is on fire. I scoop up the little hellion before opening the door.

When I open the door, Oren stands before me like I've never seen him before. Loose blue jeans, a tight white V-neck shirt, and a dazzling smile. I do believe he looks even sexier out of uniform. Then my eyes land on the large bouquet of yellow flowers he's holding.

"Olivia." He nods, shooting me a dazzling grin.

"Hey." I swat at Pedro, trying to get him to quit growling.

"I know you don't date, but," he holds up the roses, "I had to."

My face burns with embarrassment at his gesture and then everything else that happens flows out naturally, like we've been an old couple for years.

"Thank you, Oren." I bounce up on the tips of my toes, giving him a one-armed hug. Pulling away from him is a different story. He's wearing new cologne that hypnotizes me into the most sex-inducing trance ever. He smells a tad bit sweeter than his normal masculine musky smell with hints of a woody smell mixed with basil.

"Hey, killer." Oren pats the top of Pedro's head and I realize I'm still hanging off him like a freaking crazy-ass monkey.

I slowly step away, inhaling deeply, relishing the smell without flat-out sniffing him.

"This is Pedro," I say stepping back, letting Oren into my apartment.

"Seems like quite a vicious guard dog."

"He's all bark and no bite."

Oren hands me the roses and I melt when the slightest scent of him lingers on them. "Let me grab some water for our dinner roses."

I air quote the last part.

"I like the heels, Olivia."

I peer down to the damn hooker heels Scout forced on me and shyly grin.

"You look gorgeous."

"Naw..." I stop myself, remembering the speech Scout gave me earlier. "I mean thank you, Officer, and you my hot cop, clean up quite nicely too."

"Man, since moving here I've been pulling double shifts, heading home stripping down to my boxers, and then back up at it again."

I choke on my own spit, picturing him clothed only in boxers and then getting UP in the morning. Good lord, I need to get a grip.

"Whoa puppy."

I turn back to Oren just in time to get the perfect view of Pedro pounding out his own sexual frustrations at Oren's ankle. Full-out Yorkie humping like there's no tomorrow.

"Pedro, damn you." I drop the roses into a vase full of water. "Pedro."

Finally, when I reach him, I slap his little bump, knocking him out of his perfect rhythm.

"I'm so sorry, Oren. He usually is only an elbow humper."

Oren's laugh bubbles up from his chest.

"God, that didn't sound good, did it?" I stand up with the little horny humper tucked under my arm.

"You two have to be the cutest pair I've ever met." Oren steps forward, gently places his lips on my forehead, leaving behind a tender kiss before standing back up.

"Uh…" I fumble like a whore in church for my next few words. "Uh, he pisses on the people he doesn't like, so I guess you made the cut."

"I'm sorry, Olivia, I can't do this."

My heart sinks down to my toes with each of his words. I feel tears begin to pool up behind my brown eyes and wonder what in the hell I did wrong. *Did he get that offended by Pedro's actions?*

Before I muster up the courage to form a word, Oren steps in closer to me, clutches my cheek with one of his large palms, and then dips his face to mine. His gorgeous brown eyes are the last thing I see before his scent knocks all the sense out of me.

His lips grace mine, running slowly across them, and then his other hand pulls me in closer by the small of my back. Pedro remains frozen, sandwiched between us. Oren's lips press a bit harder into mine and then he swipes his tongue out along the seam of my lips. I moan with the intimate touch.

Oren deepens the kiss, pushing his tongue into my mouth and circling it and then pulls back, just focusing on my lips and peppering them with gentle kisses.

"I'm sorry. I couldn't resist. Standing here and talking to you without giving you a kiss was torture."

He keeps his hand pressed on the small of my back, keeping me upright while he tries to apologize for that.

"Oren just shut up." I hold my free trembling hand up to him. "That was the best first kiss a girl could ever ask for."

"First?" he asks stepping back, clutching the back of his hair and leaving his hands there.

I shyly nod yes.

"Shit. Olivia, you are really going to be the death of me."

I set Pedro down. The first kiss must have scared the shit out of him because he scatters away, struggling to keep his little legs under him as he scatters on the vinyl flooring.

The room spins a bit when I stand straight back up, going a bit dizzy.

"So you're okay with it?" Oren drops both of his arms. "I know you're traumatized from dating and banned it."

"Yeah, I did."

"So, what are we going to call this?" Oren steps up to me again, wrapping both of his arms low around my waist and backing me up to the counter until my calves hit the cupboards. His fingers dig into my hips as he lifts me up onto the counter. Oren settles his large frame between my legs. His hands glide and mold to the sides of my cheeks as he dips his face lower to mine.

"I think it's called kissing." I mumble into his lips. "Amazing, hot, and the best kissing in the history of all kissing by hot cops."

I feel his smile press into my lips before he begins kissing me again. He nurtures my lips with each graze of his. His taste is addictive with each peck. My palms remain planted on the counter, keeping myself steady. A warmth spreads over my body as Oren captures my bottom lip in his teeth.

He pulls back a bit. "Your turn to kiss me, Olivia."

I sit up straighter, curling my arms around my middle, crawling right back into my embarrassment shell.

"Olivia." Oren uses his forefinger to lift my chin up to him. "Kiss me please."

"I don't know how to."

His sexy smile covers his face. "Close your eyes and jump with me, Olivia."

I follow his instructions, fiddling with my fingers until he unclasps my tangled arms, placing my palms on his cheeks. With eyes shut, I lean forward until our lips touch. I fight to remember the movements of his lips and what his actions were. I lavish his taste with each peck and build up more courage with each time our lips touch.

A low groan bubbles up from his chest, giving me the courage I need to savor one final grace of his lips before pulling back.

"Best kiss ever," Oren says standing straight up. "Now, let's get you to dinner before this turns into a date."

"Roses, sweet kisses, and now dinner with a sex god is pretty much classified as a date," I reply, holding onto his shoulders to help balance myself for the leap down to the ground. I'm not sure if it's the mixture of the emotion coursing through my veins or the trashy hooker heels, but my legs wobble to the point of my knees knocking together.

Oren hooks his arm through mine. "Are you okay going on a date with me?"

"I think I am." I nod my head. "Just no pasta throwing. I mean, you did pass the Pedro test."

Oren is quite the gentleman, opening all doors for me even the one to his Jeep Wrangler, forcing me to pinch myself to wake myself up from this dream. It's all too good to be true.

"Gravy Doug's?" he asks, stopped at a red stoplight.

"Hell yes," I squeal.

"I mean, we hit it off there pretty good the first time, so I'd hate to try anything else."

"Yum and do I get to still dip your finger steaks in my gravy?"

"I guess."

Gravy Doug's is dead, which makes me happy. Less staring eyes to start the gossip circle. Oren surprises me when he slides in on my side of the booth until we are shoulder to shoulder.

"Hey there," I say with a big smile.

"You ordering for me? Set me straight on my ways at Gravy Doug's."

"Oh, I can show you the light for sure." I slide the two menus to the end of the table and then feel his hand wind into mine.

There's a new waitress who oozes a bit too much sexiness for me. I have to give it to Oren, he doesn't sneak one peek at her supple cleavage or tops of thighs in her freakin' boy shorts. Ol' Gravy Doug must be getting lonely and quite horny in his old age.

"You do like that chicken fried steak, uh?" Oren asks, squeezing my hand.

"Yeah, I'm a gravy girl." I shrug and give his fingers a squeeze.

"How in the hell have you remained single so long?"

"I'm a weirdo magnet. No offense."

Oren slowly moves his fingers in mine. The movement nearly causes me to melt into a pool of horny teacher.

"Seriously."

"I'm serious," I reply.

"Twenty questions?" he asks, raising an eyebrow.

I twist in the booth to face him. "What are the rules?"

"Anything goes."

"You get one question and then I ask you one."

"Deal." Oren takes a long gulp of his ice water. "How many boyfriends have you had, Olivia?"

"You know that answer," I reply.

"Seriously and I'm like a walking lie detector."

"Fine, one from first grade. His name was Skipper and he was imaginary."

"I knew it." He slams the table.

His deep chuckle makes the embarrassment creep up into the pinks of my cheeks.

"My turn." I reach over and grab his forearm, shocking myself at such a bold move. "How many girlfriends have you had?"

"Do you want the truth or a lie?" he asks

"Truth, Oren."

"A lot. Too many to count."

All righty then, I should've picked lie.

"College?" he asks.

"State college here in Oregon. Teaching school with Scout, lived in the dorms, watched Seinfeld every single night in my dorm room eating Fig Newtons."

"Par-tay animal."

"You know it. Okay, Oren where are you from? Where did you grow up and what brought you here?"

"Slow down, turbo, one question at a time."

"I'm boring, Oren. I was raised by my dad. No boyfriend and still have my V card. You've met Pedro and Scout, the two other people in my life beside my dad. My mom died when I was nine." I pause, thinking of anything else. "Oh, and I hate the letter O."

"Why do you hate the letter O?" He raises an eyebrow in my direction.

"Really Officer Oren O'Brien? I'm Olivia Olander who lives in Ontario, Oregon and who is O-less."

And I slap both hands over my mouth, instantly missing the feel of his hand in mine. I spread my fingers enough to talk through them. "Talk now before I die of embarrassment."

His words are laced with laughter. "I'm from Southern California and a third generation police officer. I have a big, loud family with four brothers and three sisters. And Olivia, I hated my life in California. I asked for a transfer for a fresh start. Oh, and I love the letter O."

"No more alphabet allowed in tonight's conversation and we're never playing twenty questions again."

"Deal. It's nice knowing more about you, Olivia."

"You too, Officer Hot Pants."

"You and your damn nicknames."

And the food saves the day from anymore awkward conversation. Oren's a gentleman, letting me dip in his gravy and steal bits of his food from his plate. The man can eat. He puts away all of his food plus my leftovers.

"Was it as good as the first time?" I ask and then die a bit on the inside, realizing how dirty the question could be.

"Delicious and the company just as sweet and loveable." He taps the end of my nose before he goes to pay the bill.

My heart sinks knowing our date is nearing an end. Even with the horrifying conversation, Oren has a weird way of making me feel comfortable through all of it.

"Dutch?" I ask, walking up behind him, while staring at his perfect ass.

"Not a damn chance," he says without turning around.

"I can pay my half."

"You said it was a date and that means I pay."

"Well, thank you, Oren."

He turns around, clutches my hand, and holds the door of the diner open for me. "You might not be saying thank you in a few minutes."

Chapter 10

The Reign of Hulk Hogan

I'm going to freaking murder Scout with a dull ice cream scoop. If I had my cellphone right now I'd be calling her ass up and letting her have it.

"I'm ready when you are, Olivia." Oren's voice drifts through into the dressing room.

"Just a second." I reach up behind my neck and tie off the top of my bikini. That's right, I'm standing on cold cement in a bright yellow and red bikini of Scout's at a natural hot springs at night. My breasts barely fill out Scout's top and I look like a little child dressed up in a Hulk Hogan wannabe swimsuit. Thank fuck, I'm not a natural blonde. I'm pretty sure Scout bought this swimsuit as a role-playing outfit with Taylor. *Ewwww, abort thought. Shit, fuck, bitch, that was gross.*

I swing open the dressing room door, ready to give the what for to Oren for bringing me to the local "soak and poke" pools, but him in swim trunks leaves me speechless and spasming between the legs.

He's in burnt orange swim trunks that compliment his skin perfectly and I definitely see a California man before my eyes. His abs are more chiseled than I ever imagined. But I'm hypnotized back up to his beautiful face outlined with his strong jawline, brown eyes and luscious dark hair. He has a skeptical smile covering his face.

"Are you going to kill me?" His expression turns even more worried.

"I'm going to murder Scout and then block her number from your phone and yours from hers." I plant both hands on my hips and then dash for the towel he sent me into the dressing room with. *Shit, I just probably made thousands of Asian Hulk Hogan fans scream world wide with that stance.*

"Stop." Oren grasps my wrist and pulls me towards him, letting the towel drop to the dressing room floor. "I know Scout was being a bit devilish, planning this date...I mean dinner or friend night out...Shit." Oren runs his free hand through his hair.

"Date," I correct him.

"I've heard several of the officers talk about this place and well, uh...I wanted to come here with you."

"You do know this is called the "local soak and poke", right?"

"I'm aware of how many babies have been made here. But I've never been to a natural hot springs resort at night."

"You do have those puppy dog eyes mastered."

Thoughts of how many girlfriends he's had race through my mind. He's mastered the skillful touch of getting in panties or in my case, Hulk Hogan's briefs. The picture is masterfully painted before me, breathtaking hunk standing before me, says all the right things, kisses like a god, makes me squirm more than I care to admit...then all the other women he's crushed and left spilling tears on their pillows flow into view.

He is a certified lady-killer. He takes them down one at a time with his delicious and very devilish brown eyes, then the ladies swoon to his voice, then his smell, and then WHAM the whole package and they are hook, line, and motherfucking sinker. What's left, you ask? His ding-dong in your sinkhole and like a good little twat in love, you lay down and let him take you in every single position possible, except the butt- butt in the what-what because that simply causes blindness worldwide.

"Olivia." I look up to Oren staring down at me. "We going in or not?"

"Your Twinkie is getting no where near the sinkhole, you lady killer."

His familiar rumble of a chuckle fills the air. "Would you like to swim with me or at least get into the warm, comforting water instead of the cool breeze?"

"Oren."

"Olivia." He pulls me in closer, cradling my shivering bikini clad red and yellow outfit.

"Don't break my heart."

The pads of his fingers brush away tendrils of stray hair framing my face. "I'm not here to break your heart."

I feel the stray tears stream down my face, rounding my high cheekbones, and pooling into my cleavage. "I've opened up to you more than anyone else. Don't break my heart."

It's too painful to look up to him and allow Oren to analyze or even scrutinize every single emotion streaming across my face.

"Olivia, will you jump with me?" I feel him tug us closer to the edge of the outdoor pool. The steam, smell, and feel of the natural water envelopes the both of us, as we're inches away from the steaming water.

It's the local attraction that I've heard countless stories about and now I'm tiptoeing on the edge with my prince whose promising me a future I know nothing about. My heart is screaming, as I swan dive with hot cop and my brain is sending warning flares of danger up.

I'm left with one final question. "Only if you don't break my heart, Oren O'Brien."

His strong biceps tug me just enough over the edge with him until both of our bodies collide into warm, inviting waters. I let all the negative thoughts flow out as I drown into the hopeless, dark, chocolate brown eyes that have so reassured me over the days. He didn't run when the awkwardness was on full display, he only pulled closer to me.

Holding my breath underwater, I feel his tug, and then when my almond-shaped eyes spring open, it's him I stare back at underwater. It's not Officer Ladyboner, Officer Fuck Me, or even Hot Pants, it's Oren I see reaching out for me. His large palm once again clutches around my wrist and I'm dragged directly back into his vortex as he saves me from drowning in everything of him.

I'm not covered in pasta, sauce, and/or (in my damn case) humiliation...rather bathed in Oren O'Brien, who seems desperately and hopelessly in love with my awkward Asian, Yorkie-loving, and extremely cursed ass.

I gaze at my future and hope in his brown eyes as we surface from the tempting and very warm waters that something deeper lies between us, even if it's a fling I get to tell my future grandkids about.

I'm certain in this very moment that Oren's Twinkie, beyond a shadow of a doubt, belongs in one of my orifices and in this moment it could very well be my butt-holio and life would be good.

We both begin to surface at the exact time, but being the gentleman Oren is, he shoots me up first from under the depth of the waters. I gulp, gasp, and struggle to regain my bearing after the masterpiece I was just dunked with.

We both sputter for several seconds before Oren sends me a Kane's signature headlight finger movement by his left pectoral.

For a fact, I'll be murdering Scout via a dull ice cream scooper as I stare down at my left tit floating right along between Oren and myself. *Thank fuck, for the obnoxious red and yellow bikini, I mean it has to take some attention away.*

"Miss Olander." I hear a very young and eager voice squeal while my left girl remains to peacefully float in the water between Oren and I. His hands clutch low on my ass pulling me towards him, officially smashing my tit into his wet chest and like clockwork my body sings. Slowly, I swivel towards the voice while remaining locked in Oren's grasp. He uses his large palm to shield my boobie from the view of the youngster

102

while I tuck her right back down into the Hulk Hogan.

"Amy," I feign pride and everything a first grade teacher should when I make eye contact with one my students.

"You got arrested?" Little Amy's vision goes to Oren holding me in his arms. He's kept me clutched to him, splaying out both of his palms on my belly.

"No." I wave back while plastering on my best first grade grin for the know it all.

"What are you doing then?" she squeals back, which now has the attention of the entire pool, her parents included.

"Dinner." His deep yet gentle voice whispers into my ear.

"I'm doing dinner," I holler back to her without thinking and then turn to Oren. "For the love of God, drown me."

"Is this a premeditated crime?" he asks with a light chuckle accompanying it.

"Hell yes," I groan, turning back to Amy and her family.

"Do you know how to swim?"

"Watch this, Miss Olander."

The little freaking gem rapid fires off umpteen questions before her mother finally does shut her up.

"Amy, out. Your five minutes is up. Time to go."

I'm pretty sure Amy's dad saw my tit as he hasn't taken his view from my floating boobs since the escapee accident. Amy's parents both wave good-bye as they leave the pool.

"I'm starting to see there's never a dull moment with you, Olivia."

"The universe hates me." I twirl in his arms with my own arms smooshing my boobs together to keep the babies hunkered down. "And don't complain, I do believe you touched my boob."

"Just some side boob action. That's all." He raises his hands, trying to look innocent.

Using my feet against his knees, I push off of him and begin back floating. The stars in the night sky twinkle back at me and the water next to me swooshes up over my belly and when I tilt my head to the side, Oren's swimming next to me.

"Wall," he warns.

I stand up with my toes barely touching the rough bottom cement of the pool. Oren pulls me into his chest with a quick peck to my forehead. My body reacts, wrapping my legs around his center and locking my ankles.

"As much as I want to kill Scout for this, I have to admit this has been the best date of my life."

"Mine too."

"Yeah, right; you have a lot to compare it to."

"I've had my fair share." He crooks his head to the side, "but there's something I can't get past with you, Olivia."

"You're a fool." I mimic his head tilt. "You probably look at me like a trophy. You know, racking in the v cards."

His hand snakes down to my ass and squeezes until it's painful. "If I could, I'd slap your ass for saying that. I'm not that kind of guy and Olivia you don't deserve to be treated like that by anyone, especially yourself when you think like that."

"You know I'm just always waiting for the fall out. I always have been since my mom passed."

"You deserve the best. You're gorgeous, kind, caring, and bit of a train wreck waiting to happen."

My smile widens across my face and it feels good to openly talk to him about this. I really like the feeling of genuinely smiling for the first time in a long time.

"Your smile is dangerous, Olivia."

"Oh, and thank you for the kiss." I lean in, grazing his lips with mine. "Kissing is nice. Kissing you Officer Oren O'Brien is real nice."

The warm water envelopes us, the murmurs of the few other swimmers fade away into the night, as we drift of into a dark corner of the pool locked in the most breathtaking, ovary stimulating kiss known to mankind.

Chapter 11

The Verdict's in...He's Not Gay

"So you guys just kissed?" Scout bounces up onto Dad's desk, laying down lunch for our Saturday time in the shop.

"Yes, my lord, Scout I'm not a well-rounded whore like you." I know my eyes go wide and dreamy. "I swear he melted my heart, lips, and panties just with his kisses."

"Did he at least pop some wood?" She stuffs a handful of fries in her mouth.

"I- uh...felt him."

"Thank you baby Jesus. I was beginning to the think he was too good to be straight. My damn gaydar has been off lately." She slams her greasy palm down on the desk. "How do you know he got hard?"

And just like that my best friend knows damn well she has me backed in a corner.

"O, spill it now."

"It's not like I'm the most seasoned vet when it comes to bumping uglies, Scout. But his kisses and the way he looks at me."

"I told you that I really think he's into you and if he's popping wood that's a good sign he's not batting for the other team." Scout pops a fry into her mouth.

"Keep it PG, girls. I'm here for the grub and to check on expenses." My dad sits in his favorite worn down chair, grabbing his food from Scout before I have the chance to blow the full details.

"Just talking about your daughter's date last night." She waggles her eyebrows.

"Well, she's chipper and has Pedro at her feet, so I'm guessing it went okay." He draws out his last word like he's unsure of it and waiting for the ball to drop.

"It went well, Pops, he's a great guy."

"When's the next date?" Scout asks as she dry humps her bacon cheeseburger.

"We're going to the movies tonight. He had to work today."

"And where does he work?" Dad asks.

"Oh, ol' Daddio doesn't know much about your walking daydream, this must mean it's serious," Scout taunts.

"Shut up, bitchface." I toss my boat of fries at her.

"Dammit, you girls raise my blood pressure." Dad slugs his soda. "What does he do, Olivia?"

His voice leaves no question of the fact he wants an answer. *It's his 'move your ass, Olivia' voice or I'll kick it for you.* He's never laid a hand on me, but I'd recognize his serious voice from miles away.

"He's a cop. Just moved to town."

"And she wants to hump him," Scout adds.

"Jesus." Dad finishes his burger in record time. "And when do I meet this guy?"

"Hopefully, soon, Dad." I pick at the hem of my pants. "I just don't want to jinx it or scare him away."

"I'm here for you, kid, even if this guy is the one or you end up being the crazy teacher who never marries and the town suspects lesbonic behaviors."

"She throws up when she sees puss. You're good old man." Scout pats his shoulder as he saunters from the office and back out to work. Dad's hands have always been happy when covered in oil and solving the mystery of a broken engine.

"Love both of you, crazy girls."

Once the door shuts behind him, Scout peppers me with questions.

"Is he huge or mid-size and just exactly how did you touch his pecker?"

"Scout." I sit straight up in the office chair. "He's huge like Tony the Tiger has nothing on him."

"Oh shit, he's bigger than Tony." I have Scout's full attention in this moment.

"We made out in the corner of the pool. His hands were everywhere gripping my ass, roaming up my sides; he even got side boob action. Another family hopped into the pool and we had to part. When I slid down the front of his body, I felt every inch of him and then out of nowhere, I grazed his Woodie with the back of my knuckles."

"And…"

"He's glorious and huge. We had to separate and then just swam around for a bit, but holy shit it was hot."

"He's definitely into you, O." She wraps her arms around me, plopping her ass in my lap. "It's like my baby girl is growing up."

"I think I'm falling in love with him." I lean my head on her tits.

"Your cherry is going to get popped in the very near future, but as a seasoned sex freak, just watch out for your heart, O." Scout runs her fingers through my hair.

"I want to fall hopelessly in love and then get my cherry popped."

"If I've learned one thing, O, it's that it just takes days for your who-ha to heal, but forever to cure a broken heart."

I let her words soak in. I know she's right, but I also know I've fallen for every touch and compliment from Oren. My heart's being drowned in the idea and thought of love. I know I've jumped into a dark, murky pool that I can't get enough of.

My damn phone is supposed to arrive on Monday, which it better since I feel freaking naked without it. Oren gifted me with one hell of a goodnight kiss when he dropped me off last night and promised to pick me up again at seven o'clock to go to a movie and popcorn. He vowed it would be less date-ish, but my only request was more kissing and petting. He left one hell of a kiss imprinted on my lips before turning to his car.

Now here I sit in my apartment with Pedro sleeping in my lap and remember the stinging bruise of his lips on mine. It hasn't even been twenty-four hours and I'm more than ready for another outing with Hot Cop.

It's crazy because tonight I'm not worried about my outfit, hair, or makeup; my body is just zinging to see him again.

I've showered, tossed on some clothes, light makeup, and have done nothing but picture him for the last hour while mindlessly scrolling social media and petting the sleeping dog in my lap.

An ignition of fireworks light up my apartment and they're not the sexy ones, but more of a spine chilling, rapid fire barking brought to you by Pedro. A loud knock on the door sent him into spastic barking episode.

I check the clock on my wall that has each number marked by a different muscle car, courtesy of my old man, and realize it's an hour early for our movie time.

I scoop the yapping freak up into my arms and make my way to the door, swinging it open.

"Did you happen to check your peephole?"

It's him. The Sex God. The Instant Lady Boner. Mr. Get in My Vagina Right Now.

"Hey," I barely squeak out.

"Got off early and I'd text you, but..."

"Yeah, no phone. I need to give you my home phone number."

"You have a home number?"

The look on his face cracks me up. It's shock, awe, and a twinge of disgust.

"Yeah, my dad insists since I'm so clumsy and well..."

"Ahh." He nods. "Good dad, but he should teach you about checking your peephole before slinging open your door."

I grab him by the wrist and pull him into the apartment. "No one comes here but Scout and well now you. I thought it was Miss Jackass USA since you're so early."

"No excuses." He growls out. "I've seen too much shit in my career. Check the peephole."

"Yeah, yeah, yeah." I wave him off. "But nice surprise."

"Slow day and my partner took over for me."

"Nice." I nod.

"Hey, dog." He pats Pedro, who's tucked under my arm.

"Pedro," I correct.

He plucks Pedro from under my arm and pats his head while taking a seat on the couch like this is his second home. And before long they begin wrestling. Yes, the man of my dreams is currently wrapped up in a chokehold with Pedro, growls and all.

"Drink?" I ask.

"I'm good. Do you know what movie you want to see?" Oren doesn't miss a beat while wrestling and growling back at Pedro.

"I haven't been to a movie in forever. I'm lame. I correct papers for fun." I perch on the arm of the couch near the tumbling duo. "You can pick."

"I'm in the same boat as you. I haven't been to the theatres for years."

"Here." I toss him my laptop that lands between him and Pedro. Pedro pants a bit and then nuzzles into Oren's lap while he fumbles to flip open the lid.

"I've picked the diner and basically ordered for you, so you get to pick the movie."

"Chick flick or action packed? What's your choice of poison?" Oren flips open the laptop and I offer up my password.

"I like anything," I reply, fighting the urge to curl up in his lap while he plucks in the password.

And it's like he reads my mind. Oren's large palm wraps around my wrist, dragging me into his lap. His breath tickles the tender flesh on my neck. I find it easy to melt back into him. He snakes his muscular arms around me until both of his fingers are back to the keyboard.

"Password, again?" he asks.

I swear I feel his tongue lap up and leave a fiery path of passion along my neck. I'm not sure if he really just licked my neck or if it was my wild imagination.

I repeat the password one more time, making sure he strikes each key correctly. The rainbow circle of death whirls around for seconds as everything loads.

"A guy at work is saying there's a new romantic suspense thriller type in the theatres called The Hunted. I'll check the times." Each sound and syllable produced by his throaty and sex lathed voice sends chills through my body, capturing more of my heart word by word.

"Sounds amazing." In a bold move, I turn just enough to place a quick peck on his cheek.

I feel each peck of his fingers as he types in the password. It's quite a lengthy one and in this moment I'm appreciative of that. I feel myself melt even more into his comforting embrace.

I watch as he clicks on the Internet icon. Seconds float by before a ball slapping sound interrupts our intimate moment.

It's not just a ball slapping sound but it's accompanied by a hairy visual. That visual being a hairy butthole as an Oscar Meyer wiener pummels into the ass. I see hair, balls, dick, buttthole, and then my life flash before my eyes.

Once again, Scout's death is plotted from her ingenious idea of watching porn to educate myself.

I burst from Oren's lap and I don't miss his throaty laugh as I do. I know Pedro's on my heels, but I ignore him as I slam the door to my room shut and huddle in a fetal position curled in my blankets.

I'm pretty sure watching porn online is an offense, against the law, and scrutinized by people around the world. Not only did I let my best friend search it up and me attempt to watch it, but also I left the fucking browser open on my computer.

I'm going to die of humiliation right now.

"Olivia." Knuckles rapping against my door catch my attention, but I ignore them.

"Olivia, let me in."

It's his deep, sexy voice and I muster up no courage to reply.

"I'm opening the door and pray you're not standing behind it with a blunt object, ready to kill me."

The creaking sound of the door, his footsteps, and then Pedro's nails clicking on hardwood floor follow. The bouncing on my mattress is Pedro, a motion I'm used to. Then it's the low dip of the mattress that's foreign to me. A heavy touch covers my hip.

"Olivia."

"It was Scout," I blurt.

"Olivia."

"She told me to and opened it and then my curiosity got the best of me and she even had me drown my phone in my tub." I don't pull my face from the pillows.

"Olivia."

"I don't know how to date or keep a boyfriend. Kiss, have sex, none of that I know. She's tried to teach me."

"Olivia."

"I only watched a few seconds of that before I needed to scrub out my eyeballs."

"Olivia."

"I was talking to a vibrator the other night and tried using my phone in the tub."

His hand clutches my shoulder, rolling me over. "Okay, that last part is straight comedy."

Oren's deep laughter rolls in my room as he sets me up in the bed, dragging me onto his lap. Oren brushes a tendril of hair back from my frowning forehead.

"The movie starts in forty minutes. Gives us time for a quick bite to eat."

I let out a breath of pent up frustration and inhale that amazing cologne of him.

"Olivia, can you promise me something?"

"What?" I mumble.

"Let me be the one who shows you and takes care of you."

I don't respond, move in his arms, or even make eye contact with him.

"Give us a try and don't worry about it all happening, maybe just let it try."

Chapter 12

Cookie dough, where?

"Olivia."

I turn from staring in the microwave, willing my leftover Mexican food to cook faster to Scout with her legs perched up on the table in the staff room.

"What?"

"You have to try this."

"Not a damn chance." I turn back to staring at my beans.

"Seriously, I'm going to do it with Taylor."

"That's real reassuring." I pull the steaming take out box from the microwave and sit next to her.

"Don't be a stuffy bitch since Oren promised the pot at the end of the rainbow."

"I'm not." I slap her thigh and steal a grape from her bowl. "I'm just done with your antics."

"Okay, listen. My hair stylist told me that when you cook for your loved one that you're supposed to rub it in your armpits."

"What?" I choke on the damn grape. *Karma at it's best.*

"She made cookies for her man and rubbed the balled up batter in her armpits before baking and he went wild for her. It's pheromones and your partner will ravish you."

"You're kidding me, right?"

"Nope. Another lady was getting her hair done and said the same thing. So, I'm baking cookies

118

tonight and doing it. This is the gross part; it's not like you need to be super clean it's better to have your natural oils and smell on you."

"It's official. You've lost your fucking mind, Scout."

My phone dings and Scout just rattles on.

Oren: How's it going?

Me: Going.

Oren: It's been a damn long week away

I think before I type out a text to him. I don't want to show him just how damn needy I am.

Me: I miss you.

Oren: I miss you, too.

Me: We still on for Saturday night?

Oren: Yeah, I'll be home early Saturday morning.

Me: Enjoy the Hot Cop Conference and don't be hitting on any other first grade teachers. I'm kind of fond of you.

Oren: Will do

I set my phone back down on the table and try to focus in on Scout and her latest insane idea.

"So, why would you do this? You and Taylor screw like bunnies."

She shrugs. "I just don't want to lose the spark."

"What's going on?" I push her.

"He's been distant and I know it's because both of our jobs are super busy this time of year."

"You're overthinking it. He loves you."

"Enough about me. I've got this armpit and pheromone shit under control." She shoves her sandwich in her mouth. "When you seeing Oren next?"

"He's been gone all week at a cop convention or training or some shit like that. We are going out tomorrow night after I work at my dad's shop."

"Going to slide into second base or shoot for a home run?"

"I don't know. I guess we'll take it as it comes."

The batty old third grade teacher interrupts us. "I hate to tell you, Olivia, but there's no cop training this week. That's at the end of the month."

"Oren's new so maybe it's something else the others don't do."

"Think what you want, dear."

The bell rings and the teachers begin dispersing.

"Don't listen to her." Scout pats my shoulder. "She came to school with cat shit in her hair last week."

An hour floats by and I still have a terrible feeling about her comment, so I finally text Oren at last recess. I know I'm overanalyzing everything now but I don't even know where he went or what exactly he was doing.

Me: Hey! I didn't ask you where your training was.

Oren: California, why?

Me. Oh! I collect shot glasses. Want to grab me one?

Oren: of course xoxo

Me: Thanks

His xos throw me off my game. He's back in California. I wonder if he's near his hometown. I turn to my computer and fire up Google to search cop trainings in California.

"Olivia, stop. He has nothing to lie about. Scout's right, Mrs. Donald is a dingbat," I say out loud to myself.

It takes several minutes to talk myself out of searching the conference and his names. To love is to trust and the only way to find love is to rely on trust...it's a blind leap of faith.

"He's at a conference," I reassure myself.

"Miss Olander why are you talking to yourself?"

I turn to see Janis staring at me like I've lost my marbles.

"It's what you do when you get older," I respond.

Chapter 13

Fart

"No Scout today?" Dad asks, sitting next to me.

"Nope, she's baking cookies."

"The girl doesn't know how to cook, does she?"

"Nope and she's going to rub the dough in her armpits."

"Less is more, Olivia."

"Here." I hand him a bag. "You won't like it as much as the heart attack shit Scout feeds you, but it's yummy."

He peeks into the bag and grimaces. "I'm not a damn rabbit and you know I hate eating seagull."

"Lettuce is healthy and it's chicken, Pops."

He just grunts and digs in. My dad's not one for waste and is usually hungry. He's a hard worker. The old-fashioned type; up before the dawn and working all day long. I worry about him and how long his body will hold up for him.

"I have all your May bills paid and logged. The shop is doing great."

"I can't believe May is already done. When you out for the summer?"

"June twelfth."

"Want a summer job turning a wrench?"

I laugh at him. "You ask me this every summer."

"Well, I figure one day you might take me up on it. You're all I got, girl."

"Dad, I'll always keep this shop going, even if it's not my prissy little hands twirling the wrenches."

"I know. I know. Just want to instill that in you."

A thundering engine rolls up to the front of the shop. Dad pokes his head out the door and shakes it side to side.

"Everyone in town knows I'm strict about my damn lunch break." He stands up, tossing the Tupperware container to the desk. I notice all the lite dressing and chicken is gone while a bed of perfect lettuce remains in the bottom.

He steps out of his office to face the newly arrived car. "Holy shit, now that's a car."

I peek around my dad and spot a black, sleek, and very sexy 1967 Shelby Mustang. The chrome shines in the daylight.

"Well, if this isn't better than any damn shitty salad."

I pat my Pop on the shoulder. He's a car lover at heart and oldies are his favorite. I turn to go back into the office and offer Pedro some of my chicken off my salad and dump Dad's greens into my bowl and combine it all together.

I hear Dad's voice off in the distance talking to the customer and go right back to finishing up the books for the month, so I can go home and wait on my own personal sex god or at least I hope one day he earns that title.

I turn the music up on the docking station and rock out to the best of the nineties. For years, my dad scolded, persisted, and damn near arm-wrestled me into going into the accounting field. I love working with numbers, it's mindless, and soothing to me, but I knew I'd miss the human interaction part of it. I guess I went whole hog diving into the teacher world.

I lift one butt cheek off the chair and rip some wind. Pedro barks, getting caught off guard.

"It's just me, boy, being so damn lady like." I roll my eyes and tidy up my work area.

That damn chicken I think to myself as I hike my leg, steadying myself to rip another one. It's the loudest fart I've ever heard, causing the whole area of butt to vibrate. When you begin to giggle at your own farts you know you're a teacher. I'm damn tempted to go for a third one, but the possibility of sharting is lingering on the horizon.

"Olivia."

I swivel in the office chair to see my dad and motherfucking Oren standing just inside the office. *Maybe they didn't hear it.* I feel the blood drain from face and my fingers shake with the possibility of embarrassment. *Dear Farting gods please help a little innocent Fart Loving god woman like me.*

"What do you think about that damn rabbit food now you keep trying to stuff down my throat?" My dad asks and then proceeds to bust out into a belly laugh to the point he has to rest his palms on his knees all hunched over.

I slap both of my palms over my mouth and want to scream fuck you to the Farting gods of the Earth.

"Olivia." Oren's voice carries the natural deep husk to that sends chills up my spine. It's saying a lot in this epic time of embarrassment. I can only manage to nod back to him.

Dad finally is able to stand up after several minutes of howling like a hyena. "You know my daughter?"

I bite down on the inside of my cheek, wondering how in the world this could possibly get any more awkward.

"Yes, sir, I do." Oren looks my dad straight in the eye when he talks.

"How?" Pops counters.

Oh, shit. He's about to bear his protective dad teeth to Oren.

I'm still paralyzed from humiliation to even drop my hands from my mouth and help Oren out of my dad's interrogation.

"I visited her class during career week representing Orange County Police."

"You are." Dad pauses looks at me and then back to Oren and raises his pointer finger. "You're Mr. Lady Boner?"

Oh, for fucksake!

"Scout?" Oren asks my dad.

"Yep. I try to avoid her and Olivia's conversations, but always find myself walking in on them at the worst times."

"Oren O'Brien." He sticks his hand out to my dad.

"Olivia's dad or also known as Pops."

The men do the manly handshake and nod heads before turning back to me with my hands still covering my mouth.

"Olivia, we came in here because I'm out of work order sheets in the garage. Could you grab me a few?"

I stand from the chair, remove my hands from my mouth, and finally discover my voice through the ocean of humiliation. "Pops, Oren is the guy I've been dating."

The word dating feels weird rumbling off my tongue especially in front of my dad and Oren.

"Yeah, I figured as much since he's Mr. Lady Boner."

"Dad. Enough," I spat and turn to grab him a stack of papers. "Here you go."

"Open a window or something Olivia, I haven't replaced the batteries in the carbon monoxide detector in a couple of months."

Both men erupt in a knee slapping laughter that last moments longer than it should. The embarrassment fades away since this is the first time the two men in my life are in the same room and also sharing a moment. Even if that moment is over my reckless flatulence.

"I'll go grab that VIN number and look up the parts." Dad pats Oren on the shoulder and strolls away.

Oren takes a step closer to me. "Nice guy."

"I get all my charm from him. What can I say?" I shrug my shoulders.

"Always full of surprises." He draws out the full for a bit too long.

"Not one word of this." I hold a finger up to him. "If Scout gets wind of this she'll have it engraved on my headstone."

He grabs my wrist, tugging me into him. "I won't blow your secret, baby."

"Oren." I slap his wrist and let a giggle escape because not even Strawberry Shortcake could make this one up.

"I missed you way more than I thought possible." He bends down and gently kisses me. He doesn't let his lips linger on mine or dart his tongue into my mouth.

"I really missed you, like stalker criminal missed you."

"Good to hear." His smile widens, but he remains standing.

"What conference did you go to again?"

"Orange County doesn't have a certified criminal detective and I was one back in California, so just had to go back and extend the certification."

"Wow. Fancy." I stand on my tiptoes and peck his lips. "Anyone else from the force go with you?"

"No. My partner tried so he'd get a good vacation out of it but the chief didn't go for that."

I kiss him again and feel him stiffen.

"It's not you, Olivia. Your dad." He nods back towards the shop.

"You're such the gentleman," I taunt. "But can we get to second base tonight? My ovaries are about to combust just smelling you."

"You smell me?" he asks with a scrunched up brow.

"I'll admit it sounds a bit creepy when I say it out loud, but yeah you're my favorite scent." I kiss him on his tender lips again. "I need an Oren candle to burn in my house."

"Looks like I can get your baby up and running again like a champ. Just a week to get the parts in."

Oren turns to my dad while still holding my hand. "Great. I can't believe that engine started knocking. Can you park her here until you get her fixed?"

"Sure, no problem." Dad turns to me. "Olivia, you should've told me your man is into old cars."

"Pops, I didn't know and your reference is creepy."

"Fine, you should've told me Mr. Lady Boner was into old cars."

"Okay, abort. Dad, just call him Oren, please."

I unwind my fingers from Oren's and snag my purse and Pedro.

"She didn't know about my car. I had to go back to California for re-certification this week and swung by, grabbing my last few things from my parent's house."

"So, you making this Oregon gig your permanent one?" Dad asks him. I mentally give him a high five.

"Yeah, I really like it here and there was no opportunity for me back home to climb the ranks and make a name for myself." He pauses and looks over to me, giving me all sorts of goose bumps where I didn't even know you could get them. "And I'm pretty fond of Pedro here."

Oren grabs Pedro from under my arm and all my worries about him not working while in California fade away. He's answered every single question of mine and it also makes sense that he flew there and drove back in his car.

Oh, lordie that car gives me sexy-ass vibes just looking at it and now knowing Oren is the stud behind the wheel, I'm a worthless fangirl as I pass it in the garage.

"I was going to walk home, but since you're here…"

"What? Just say it."

I pause, giving him the sideways look.

"You know that you're just dying for a ride in my practical, safest mid-size SUV on the market, right? I mean, it is equipped with six airbags."

"Told this damn girl she could have any car when she graduated college, but her choice of a Challenger went out the door. I see too many horrible wrecks in those cars."

"I agree with your dad, Olivia."

"Okay, Mr. Safety Pants."

I can already tell these two could get along very well if they had the chance. Their friendship would blossom over their sole purpose of harassing me.

"Get in or hoof it," I tell Oren and then turn to kiss my dad. He always gives me a one-armed hug.

"Love you, Firework, be safe."

"You got it, Old Man." I toss my purse in the backseat and go to climb into the driver's seat. Oren and Pedro are already seated in the passenger seat, looking out the window.

"Olivia."

I turn to my dad, who's standing at the entrance of his shop, wringing his hands with his old-stained rag. As I get older, I recognize all the signs of the years wearing down on my dad and it makes my heart sad. His wrinkles deeper, body moving slower, and balding head; all the tell-tell signs that my dad isn't the invincible Hulk that I've always pictured him to be.

"Yeah, Pops." I have one leg in the car and palms on the top of the door.

"I'm really proud of you. I think you've found it." He sends me a wink.

"I love you."

He gives me one final wave of his rag before he turns back to his shop and I know the "it" is the magical love him and Mom found. Above all of Scout's advice, my insecurities, and worries, my dad's approval cemented everything for me. I plop down in my seat and look over to Oren, who's avoiding Pedro. He is intent on humping Oren's elbow...I'll give this everything, even if it means years of healing a broken heart because the promise of something bigger is worth it to me.

"Where to, mister?" I ask as I pull out of the garage.

"Good girl."

"What?" I ask.

"You buckled up."

"Oh good gravy, maybe dating a cop isn't the best idea."

"God, you're gorgeous, Olivia."

"Was it the massive eye roll or these ratty jeans that convinced you?"

"I think I fell harder for you when I found out you fart louder than me."

I slam on the breaks at a stop sign. "Not another word about that, Oren."

I point my finger into his chest. His swift hand grabs my wrist and pulls me towards him. His lips are on mine, devouring them before I can make another death threat. Oren is aggressive this time, biting at my lips and kissing me like his life depends on it.

"Fuck, I needed that." He mumbles into me and then sits back into his seat, adjusting his jeans.

I focus on nothing else but the road as I just drive. I have no idea where I'm going and can't even find the common sense to ask. Oren takes a couple calls while I drive. We end up at Oskar Lakes, which is a large wildlife preserve with fishing ponds, walking trails, a picnic area, and play area for youngsters.

"Olivia, I need to make one more call. Are we walking the dog or something?"

"Sure." I shrug.

He slams the door to my car, causing me to jump. His actions seem angry but nothing else about him does. I fiddle with Pedro's harness while he bounds into the window, trying to escape. I wonder if he'll ever act like other dogs.

Oren's voice raises outside the car. I can spot him in my side mirror. The veins in his neck pop with anger as his voice keeps getting louder and louder. I try to decipher the words, wondering what in the hell could have him so upset, but then Pedro spots another dog and lights up the inside of the car with his high pitched, rapid fire streams of barking. It's a hopeless cause because he thinks he's ten feet tall and bulletproof and will attack another dog.

I finally clip the leash to his harness decorated with pork chops and open the door. By the time I make it to Oren, he's tucking his phone into his back pocket.

"Everything okay?" I ask.

"Yes." He kicks up dirt. "No."

"I'm sorry." I wrap my arms around his midsection, holding onto the base of the leash and letting Pedro roam. "Anything I can do?"

"It's fucking complicated," he growls, wrapping both of his arms around me and kissing the top of my head. "It's my mom. My family has serious issues."

"I'm sorry."

"No, I'm sorry. You had to hear that."

"Well, I didn't hear much. Pedro went ape shit crazy over another dog."

His chuckle makes me feel lighter. "Good."

"I'm guessing it's one of the reasons you moved."

"Yeah, one of them."

"Oren you've seen me in more than my fair share of embarrassing moments. Talk to me."

We walk down a graveled path in silence for a few minutes before Oren grabs my hand and we settle down on a picnic bench.

He shrugs his shoulder a couple of times and acts like he's going to talk, but nothing ever comes out.

"You've seen me at my worse, Oren. Just give me the short version if it makes you feel any better."

"Why are you so persistent on this, Olivia?"

"Because." I swivel on the bench, straddling it and scooting as close as possible to him. "I know nothing about you besides the fact you're a hot cop from California. A seriously hot cop."

I waggle my eyebrows at him trying to lighten the mood, but it's the truth. It's all I know of the man.

"My parents are very concerned about outward appearances. Their house could be burning down and they'd convince you everything is going just peachy." Oren pauses, so I grab his hand and give it a gentle squeeze. "I was raised around a lot of money. My parents are high society and had set rules of how our lives would go. We were to be the best at everything. It's just lucky I love law enforcement since I had to follow my dad's footsteps. I got tired of all their shit and the fact they never let me live life, so I left."

My heart sinks in my chest. "They want you to come home?"

I can't muster up the courage needed to look him in the eye and confirm my worse fear. This is my home and I'd never leave my dad.

"Oh mommy dearest is demanding it, threatening me with my inheritance. I've heard it time and time again, Olivia. You have no idea how shallow they are. I had to escape. I couldn't even breath under their control."

"That sucks, Oren." I keep my gaze locked on our intertwined fingers.

"My younger brother puts up with their shit doing exactly as he's told. Dating the girls with the looks and right names. He's mindless and loves their control. Me, on the other hand, I've always butted heads with them. I'd sneak off to the beach and hang out with the friends I wanted."

I finally look up to him. "So, you're the black sheep of the family?"

He nods and then pulls his hand from mine, cupping my cheek and leaning in until our lips touch. "Olivia, stop worrying. I'm not going anywhere and I'm sure as hell never going back home."

"How can you know that?" I ask brushing his lips with each word.

"Because everything I want I'm holding right now and nothing will pull me from it."

I respond with a kiss that eases my heart and nerves. Several people pass us on the trail so I make it a quick one.

"I'm sorry they treat you like that," I offer.

"I'm not, Olivia. It brought me to you."

"When you put it that way. I agree."

"Thanks for making me open up to you, Olivia.

"Your welcome and thanks for sharing, now let's go make out under that tree over there." I point to a line of trees bordering the lake.

"Mmmmm. I get to make out with a hot teacher."

"We are quite the pair," I say with a giggle.

Pedro happily trots out in front of us as, hand in hand, we find the perfect tree to settle under. A blanket would be nice, but I'll take Oren.

He's the first to sit down and I settle right next him. Within seconds he has me straddling his lap and facing him. He brushes back the long hair framing my face and puts his lips on mine. I do believe kissing is my new favorite extra-curricular activity. My arms easily wrap around his neck, sealing me closer to him. Oren's lips work me over with each kiss, lick, and nip of his teeth. His large palms sneak up the back of my shirt to my bare skin.

I moan into his mouth with his touch and begin moving my hips back and forth without realizing I'm doing so. His fingers dig into my back while he deepens the kiss. I find myself exploring his sweet mouth with my tongue and being bold and brazen as I do. With thrust of my hips, I feel him through my jeans, and by him I mean his Tony the Tiger.

"Fuck, Olivia," he huffs out and pulls back.

"What?" I ask with concern.

"I'm having a hard time containing myself here. Thank God we are out in public."

His hands move from by back and lace into my hair, tugging it back and finding the exposed part of my neck. He trails kisses up and down the tender flesh and then ducks his head lower and bites my hardened nipples through my shirt.

It sends an electrifying thrill through my body, causing me to moan even louder and pushing my chest into his face. I wrap my hands around the back of his head, urging him on. My shirt is pulled up and then it's just the thin layer of my lacy bra he bites through.

"Oren." It's a breathy plea.

"Here." He sets me next to him and then lays back, pulling me with him.

I peek up to Pedro, who is snoozing and soaking up all the sunrays. Oren tugs me in close to him, positioning me towards the trees, away from the public.

"What?" I ask, intrigued with Oren's next action.

"Do you trust me, Olivia?"

I shrug. "Just kidding. Yes."

"Want your first O?" he asks.

"Here?" I squeal and sit up in a flash. My forehead slams into his as I spring upwards.

He rubs his forehead. "Not sex, but let me show you how it feels. It's like an appetizer of things in your very near future."

The promise in his voice hypnotizes me into a lusty induced coma where I'd do anything this man asked me to. Oren nudges me back into the grass, while covering the side of my body with his. The sound of my zipper going down is loud and causes me to clam up. Oren must sense it, so he covers my lips with his, swallowing all of my worry.

I concentrate on his kiss, smell, and embracing touch but feel his roaming hand sneaking under my panties. In one second, I'm a worried mess and then the next Oren makes it all disappear with his lips.

His fingers dance under my panties until they reach my...holy shit my magic button. Oren smiles on my lips when he feels my deep intake of breath on his mouth, but he doesn't slow his fingers as they move around down in my jeans. My brain becomes foggy as he strikes more pleasure with a swirl of his finger. The building tension in my belly fills until I have to pull away from his lip and arch my head back into the grass.

Oren doesn't halt the rhythmic movement as he continues to stroke me. With each movement, I buck back up into him, hanging on for dear life. It's an intense sensation I've never experienced. Moan after moan escapes me as his fingers work faster and push deeper into my flesh.

My own fingers dig into the earth below me, tearing at the grass, and then pulling it up as I explode and see stars under the touch of Oren. When I open my eyes, I see Oren staring back down at me with a mischievous grin covering his face.

"That's what it feels like?" I ask, still riding out his hand.

I should be embarrassed, humping his hand and talking to him, but the sensation and emotion rolling through me nulls everything else out. I only see and feel him.

Oren pulls his hand from me, oddly making me feel naked and bared to the world without his touch. He then gives me the show of his life, dipping his fingers that were just in me into his mouth, licking them clean.

"Like, I said, it's just an appetizer of what's to come, Olivia."

Chapter 14

School's Out For The Summer

Oren: What time is the BBQ today?

Me: 11:20 in about forty-ish minutes I get to smell you!

Oren: That's an early lunch

Me: I teach first grade...they have little bellies

Oren: Can I show up in my uniform?

Me: Pretty Please

Sleeping at night has proven difficult without the touch of Oren. We've never stayed over night at my place. I've never seen his. However, the man has morphed me into a lip-locking queen. He's pleasured me with his fingers, lips, and everything in between besides the big dirty deed.

It's saying a lot since we've both been slammed with work and have little time together. Wrapping up a school year is torture on steroids and Oren's been filling in his new position at the station. He tried explaining to me one night about the detective of something or something, but his lips were just too damn distracting to pay attention.

All I know is he's a fantastic cop who does his job well. I've seen him with his lights on pulling over several members of the community. I don't spot him on the road much as his job is morphing more into an office detective type. Shit, I don't know. I just know after weeks of being with him I'm ready for the whole kit'n caboodle.

"So, Mr. Hot Pants is coming to the barbecue today?"

The voice streaming in my room causes me to leap into the air, knocking my knee on my desk, streams of curse words flowing from my mouth as I vigorously try petting the pain from my knee.

"Busted you sexting again!" Scout sings as she plants her ass on the corner of my desk. Then she busts into "School's Out For the Summer."

"I swear you have ninja like stalking tendencies."

"Naw, it's not that hard when you're staring at your cell phone like it's a big piece of chocolate cake."

"Butthole. And yes he's still coming to the barbecue."

"I'm telling you, O, that man is a keeper." Scout snatches up the half eaten candy bar on my desk. "He puts up with you and Pedro, takes you to dinner every week at your favorite diner whether he's on shift or not, and now is coming to the end of the year barbecue."

"He's pretty awesome." My voice is dreamy and laced with lust. It happens every single time I talk to Scout about him.

"The guy has it bad for you if he's willing to come eat an overcooked paper thin patty with a stale bun and a side of first grade snot."

It's definitely odd for Scout to be talking about me and Oren more than her last rambunctious sexual encounter with Taylor. I'm pretty sure they've exhausted every single position, device, and toy.

"Is Taylor coming?" I regret it the moment the question leaves my mouth.

"No." Her face grows sad and then huge tears begin streaming down her cheeks.

"Scout." I'm up and on my feet at her side, hugging her. The only time I can remember her crying is when she lost the after school fight to Scotty McLockit in fourth grade. She landed a few a good punches, but then he rang her bell.

"He left me."

"What?" I grip her shoulders and make her face me.

"I found out he was cheating and I wanted to make it work, but he left."

"What?" I yell louder this time. "Why haven't you told me this?"

"You're finally having your moment in life and I didn't want to ruin that for you."

"I'd smack you hard if you weren't crying." The truth is, she's breaking my heart in this moment.

"It just happened last week. I knew things were off."

"Where is he?" I ask. "I'm going to beat his ass."

Scout laughs into my shoulder, drying her tears. "Oh yeah, O, I bet he'd be real scared of you."

"Fucker should be. He broke your heart."

"It's like I said, O, it takes time to get over a broken heart, but you'll never know it's worth it until you're all in."

"I'm so sorry Scout." I pet her hair, hugging her, and rocking back and forth.

"I'm going to bat for the other team. I've already Googled lesbo bars in our area."

141

"Stop, you just need time."

I've been through several of Scout's break-ups. Days on end of junk food, chick flicks, take-out, and lots of tears, but this time I wasn't there. Then the guilt hits; I'm happy right now living on cloud nine.

"Olivia, stop. I can practically hear your guilt screaming from your thoughts."

I know this is different for many reasons. One being Oren and the second one is, I really thought Taylor was the real deal. They'd been ring shopping, moved in together, and were inseparable.

"After I check out today, I'm going home for a few weeks, so don't worry about me."

"I'll be over to keep you company."

"Only a couple times, O, you need to be with Oren, living life."

"Did I hear my name?"

We both look up from our embraced hold to see Oren in the doorway in his sleek uniform and well-styled hair. My vision flicks up to the clock and see the minutes have flown by. Scout wipes the tears from under her eyes and then faces the wall opposite of Oren.

He picks up on the situation and instantly turns to walk back out the room.

"Stay, Oren, we have to go get our kids in about five minutes." I walk over to him and have to restrain from kissing the hell out of him.

"Is she okay?"

I nod yes, but whisper no. He mouths sorry.

"Don't be. It won't be the last time you walk in on us like this." I pet his shoulder, remembering how sexy he is topless. "Broken heart."

Scout bounds past us, recovering like a champ; it's what she does. "I'll see you guys outside."

Once she's out of earshot, I tell Oren. "I want to kill him or at least chop his nuts off."

"What have I told you about premeditated crime?"

"Seriously, he cheated on her, she wanted to fix it, then he left her."

"Relationships are hard and not everything is cut and dry."

"So, you're defending him?" I bristle up.

He grabs my shoulders, squaring me up to him. "In no way am I saying that. What I'm trying to say is that maybe Scout is better off without him."

"I really thought he was the one for her."

He shrugs. "This is the guy whose cousin had pasta tossed on you, right?"

I begin locking the door and only answer with a nod.

"Hey, I like him because it got me into your pants quicker."

I turn in a flash to him to find his devilish jokester smile on his face. "I'm kidding, Olivia. Not about liking him or in your pants, but bringing us together more than we were already drawn together."

"What happened to whose pants?" We both turn to see Kane in the hall holding a pink ticket.

"What are you doing, Kane?" I push past Oren.

"Got a pink slip."

143

"I see that." Raising an eyebrow. "For?"

"That mean third grade teacher yelled at a bunch of us and she gave me this."

"Who else got one?"

"Just me."

My blood instantly boils. One, it's the last day of school for shit's sake and two, Kane is one of those students teachers easily target in situations like this.

"I swear Miss Olander, I didn't do anything. A bunch of second graders found a cat on the playground and were holding it under a sprinkler."

I kneel down, so I'm on his level. "We've talked about this, Kane. Was something happening that wasn't right?"

He nods. *I hate damn cats and probably would've been one of the kids tormenting it.*

"Did you stand up for the right thing?"

He shakes his head side to side, his lower lips trembling. "But I didn't do it. All I did was laugh and I'm real sorry about that Miss Olander."

I take the pink slip from this hand wad it up, step in the classroom and toss it in the bin. It's one of the few times I've gone against another teacher, but will always fight for my students, even if it's the one who's given me an ulcer over the course of the year.

Oren gives me a sideways look as I shut the door behind me and grab Kane's hand.

"No principal's office today or lunch detention. You'll be eating outside with the rest of the school, Officer Oren, and myself."

"I promise that I just laughed. I'm sorry, teacher."

I ruffle his hair. "I probably would've laughed too, buddy."

Oren muffles a laugh of his own, behind a cough as Kane grabs his hand and we walk outside to the barbecue. It's a bright, beautiful day with lots of vibrating energy zooming around everywhere. I pull down my Ray Bans and search for my class lined up. They just finished up the last carnival and recess put on by the parent teacher association.

"They're over there, Miss Olander." Kane nods with his head towards the end of the pavement, near the swings.

"Thanks, buddy."

Oren stops walking and kneels down by Kane. "You know what, buddy?"

"Uh."

"We're not all given equal playing fields but it's our actions that shape us. You're lucky to have a teacher who believes in you."

"Yeah, I'm gonna miss her and I know about playing fields because my sister always talks about getting to home base."

The horrifying look on Oren's face sends me into a fit of giggles. I fight to talk between laughter. "He has a high school sister."

"Kane, I gave you a pink slip. Get inside." The shout is so loud it stops everyone in their tracks. It's time I go head to head with Mrs. Cat Shit in the Hair.

"Officer Oren, can you take Kane over to join the rest of the class and line them up for the lunch line?"

The overweight, squatty, greasy-haired, Mrs. Donald charges me. I know she won't back down and is hell bent on bullying me, so I walk to the grill where our principal is flipping burgers. She's right on my heels, foaming at the mouth.

"Why is Kane out here?" she asks, gaining the attention of Mrs. Williams, our principal.

"Why didn't the rest of the students get pink slips?"

She avoids my question. "That's not the point. He needs to be in the office for lunch detention."

"I don't agree."

"What is going on?" Mrs. Williams asks, wiping her hands on the front of her apron and turning to both of us.

Cat shit blurts before I have the chance to speak. "I gave Kane a pink slip. That boy needs to be whipped into shape before he gets to me in third grade."

"I threw it away and brought him out here with me. It was unnecessary and he was the only one to get one out of a group of boys."

"I said no one in the office today," Mrs. Williams who's always professional and stern states. "Thank you for bringing him out here, Olivia, this is a day of celebration for the students and teachers."

She goes back to cooking with the vice-principal and other office staff. I use one of Kane's signature moves, but peer around making sure no one else sees me. I hold one fist up and use my other hand in a winding motion until my middle fingers is fully saluting her and then march off to find my class.

I will make it my mission to be teaching third grade by the time Kane gets there. It will be hell or high water.

"Miss Olander!" a choir of little voices yell. I shade my eyes and then spot my little group waving like mad. Amy is in the front of the line leading while Oren is in the back following her instructions. It makes me laugh. Even from the back of the line he has them all lined up with plates and plastic ware and even half through the first part of the line.

"Thanks," I whisper, clutching my pinky to his.

"Everything okay?" he asks.

I nod, not going into detail seeing Kane right in front of him.

"I'll go to the front of the line and get my plate, then pick a spot in the grass for the class to sit."

The last day of school usually generates a weird storm of emotions ranging from anxiety to excitement. Anxiety and sadness of letting my students go and excitement for my freedom. It's something I can't explain, but I've experienced the last three years. Oddly, today it's just excitement filling me from head to toe and that reason is Oren O'Brien; I have someone this summer besides Pedro and Scout.

I find the perfect sunny place for the class and the students start sitting next to me. A couple of the girls decide it would be best if girls sat on one half of the circle and the boys on the other with the "Occifer" as most of them pronounce it.

I let them have their fun and don't set up much of any structure in the celebration of the last day. I notice Kane is hot on Oren's heels and makes sure to get the piece of grass right next to him. The next four and half minutes are peacefully quiet as the little ones chow down on their hot dogs or hamburgers, chips, and potato salad.

I nibble on my overdone burger, but stare at Oren most of the time, watching him eat just as quickly as the students. He's always so good with the kids. Soon a game of Duck Duck Goose breaks out and our little group merges with Scout's class, who is all finished up eating. We had a reading partner day with her class every Wednesday, so the students know each other quite well.

"Want mine?" I offer Oren my plate. He's out of breath and finally gave up on the game since each kid kept picking him.

"Yes, I'm starving. That meal did nothing for me."

Scout laughs out loud. "You know what they say about men with big appetites, right?"

"Scout," I warn her.

"What?" Oren smirks with a dab of mustard on the corner of his lips. He's totally intrigued to hear the answer.

"I hear," she plucks at the wrapper on her water bottle, "I hear they have big appetites."

My tensed up butt cheeks relax. I've come a long way but discussing and joking about Oren's dick size at the end of the year barbecue is way off my comfort radar.

We all share a laugh. Oren polishes off the plate and then joins in on a game of shooting hoops with some older students.

It's the perfect wrap to a school year that brought me more surprises than I ever anticipated and just the beginning to finding THE BIG O with Oren.

The End

Just kidding, my story isn't over yet! My fairytale has just begun.

Chapter 15

My Little Pony For The Win

Dear Diary,

The time has come to have dinner at Dad's with the boyfriend. Yes, I said boyfriend. I openly call Oren boyfriend. It's like I leaped out of the closet. I'm not ashamed or insecure of who I am anymore. Oren's brought out the inner girl in me. We are three weeks into the best summer ever.

Love, O

PS- I still have my V card.

"Hey, Pops." Oscar yaps and bites at Oren's ankles as we enter the foyer.

"In the kitchen, Olivia."

I clutch to Oren's hand and guide him through my childhood home. He has Pedro the psycho under one arm. Pedro and Oscar have a love hate relationship at best. One minute they're playing, then fighting, and then dry humping each other.

"You can set him down," I say to Oren.

"They're not going to kill each other?" he asks, protecting Pedro in his arms.

"Naw, they love to hate each other."

"Steaks are on, kids. Scout and her family are already in the backyard." Dad rounds the corner in one of the few thousands aprons I've gifted him with on Father's Day. "Beer, Oren?"

"Nice to see you too, Pops." I let go of Oren's hand and wrap my dad up into a hug.

I can't remember the last time we had dinner at our house instead of Scout's. Dad's chipper, moving about the kitchen, and handing Oren his favorite beer, Miller Genuine Draft. I don't attempt to tell my dad that Oren's more of a Crown Royal guy.

My sexy boyfriend rolls up the cuffs of his baby blue button shirt and pops a top with my dad. He's dressed in a casual sexy fashion in khaki shorts, a button up, and flip-flops. He has every single one of my nerves on high alert right now, making it very freaking awkward in the house I was raised in.

Oren and Dad fall into easy conversation about his baby aka his car. I swear I see my dad's chest puff out when Oren tells him it runs better than it ever has. I leave the two to chat it up about cars, engines, and all things oil related. The backyard is gorgeous in full bloom with Dad's flowers and sprouting garden.

"The hooker is here," Scout announces.

Neither her mom or dad laugh or roll their eyes because it's Scout. If she would've called me by name then we all would've been concerned.

"Hey."

I give all three of them a quick hug and pour myself one of Scout's margaritas, taking the seat next to her.

"What's been keeping you busy?" I ask her.

"Netflix and Oreos."

"Impressive," I mock.

"And you?" she asks, raising her drink to her lips.

"Just enjoying the sunshine," I reply.

"And by sunshine, you mean dick."

I don't even try to scold her and down my first tart and delicious margarita. Her mom takes care of it, threatening to wash her mouth out with soap. If I had an orgasm for every single time her mom threatened Scout with this I'd be a well-laid whore.

Dad and Oren bust out the backdoor still deep in conversation. Pops now has given Oren a second beer as he's holding two now. My heart is content watching the two of them from afar. It's picture perfect and my future.

Scout's dad gets up and joins the men, which I'm sure is to avoid the two women in his life arguing. Life feels so right in this moment I can hardly stand it.

"You still a virgin?" I whip my head towards Scout, but know it didn't come from her. Her mom has her head tilted to the side, waiting for an answer. I pour myself another drink before answering her.

"So?" Scout drums her nails on the glass top of the patio set.

"We haven't yet." An instant brain freeze hits me as I down over half the glass of yummy goodness.

"Why?" Scout and her mom both fire off in unison.

I only shrug. "We've been dating and getting to know each other."

"Oh, I'd show that boy the ropes," Scout's mom says with a dreamy look in her eye. I don't miss the fact she's staring at Oren, who's still near the grill with the guys. He's beyond dreamy with his dark brown hair, brown eyes, well-built body, and all-

American good boy looks. He's a walking and talking Captain America.

"You're waiting to fall in love aren't you?" Scout asks.

I nod. "And I've fallen head over heels for the man."

"Then?" she pries.

"I'm letting him set the pace."

"Shit. I'm going to have to pull out all the toys tonight," Scout's mom huffs out, kicking her sandal up on the table. "He's handsome and a gentleman. They don't make 'em like that anymore, Olivia, he's a keeper."

"No shit, she's right. I've been on Tinder and it's just jam packed with creeps."

"You're already on Tinder?" I ask, shocked.

"Yeah, I saw fuckface out with his new woman and figured I need some damn arm candy pronto."

"Oh, Scout." Her mom pats her forearm. "You are an idiot."

"I agree with your mom. Just let it happen."

Before either of us have a chance to harass Scout further, the men join us. Pops with a plate of piping steaks and Scout's mom jumping to uncover her famous macaroni salad and a few others, I scoot the chair out for Oren to sit by me and he does.

"Your dad won't quit giving me beers."

"I've downed three margaritas now courtesy of Scout and inquiring minds."

Oren leans over and kisses my forehead. Silence bathes the table and I know all eyes are on us. "Thank you."

153

Oren's never extended an explanation on his family situation and I know it means a lot to him bringing him to my home. I warned him about our modge podge situation and he never blinked an eye before throwing himself into our vortex.

"I love you," I whisper into his ear. It's the first I've spoken those three words to him and it only seems perfect in this situation set in the backyard I grew up in.

All eyes hone in even more on us and I feel Oren squeeze my hand. He doesn't need to answer me back. He's the reason I was brave enough to let the words slip off my tongue.

Dad passes the steak around and just like any other night when our families come together, we all fall into a comfortable conversation. The food is delicious and the drinks float around the table. Dad makes sure Oren's beer bottle never goes empty. It's the happy pitch to his voice and the giddy-up in his go that I know he's prouder than a pig in shit.

"Next week is our annual camping trip," Pops announces.

"I hear the fishing is like no other this year up in the mountains," Scout's dad replies, slugging his beer and then belching.

The conversation rolls on and then the awkward silence moment ensues as all eyes are on us once again.

"Olivia." Dad strums the side of his beer bottle.

"I'll be there. It's tradition, right?"

As if kittens were being slayed and unicorns dehorned, the atmosphere morphs into an alien anal situation.

Dad nods as his nails strum the bottle faster as the rest of the audience is on the edge of their seats.

"I'll bring the s'mores stuff like always."

And then the cat and mouse game ensues, I just wait for the first one to take the bait. Scout's mom is out as she excuses herself, taking everyone's plate into the house and starts dishes.

Dad starts several sentences and never is able to finish any of them. I had my money on Scout and she comes through like a true thoroughbred champ.

"Okay, is Mr. Lady Boner camping or not? I mean, like how serious is this shit?" Scout crosses her arms and stares me down. "I mean, is he in or not?"

Scout knows damn well her question leads in so many other directions, but her don't give a shit attitude screams across the table.

"No hablo Inglais, Culo."

"I teach fifth grade and listen to Pitbull. I'm fully aware that culo means asshole."

"Good job, asshole." I smirk back at Scout, tossing a stray olive from my plate.

"I took the week off. Olivia invited me awhile back."

"Jerk." I elbow Oren in the ribs. "We had them going."

"It was making my eye twitch how awkward it was becoming."

"Deal." Pops slaps his hand down on the table. "I'll get our camper rigged up for all three of us."

Shit, fuck, bitch. Well no dunking the doughnut with Oren in the wilderness will be happening now.

Oren squeezes my hand under the table with more force this time. I swear he's not a cop, but a damn mind reader. I down a few more drinks until Scout and her family skidaddle back home leaving Oren, Pops, and myself under the stars. Scout's mom has cleaned everything, even tidying the grill area. The woman is amazing.

Pops and Oren talk about old cars, engines, and everything else between brake pads. Pops even engages in an argument about the car Oren patrols in.

"Boys, I'm going to check on the dogs. Anyone need anything?" I stand from the table and step towards the lit back porch.

"Two more brewskis for the boy and I."

"Got it, Pops, two kicks to Oscar and two more beers coming right up." I make my way to the back porch, but don't miss a word he speaks.

"She hates that damn dog. I know I should, shit he's bit me a dozen times when I've tried saving his ass, but Oscar filled that spot when Olivia moved out, you know."

Oren's baritone voice floats away in the night sky when I swing open the backdoor. Both dogs are knocked out in Pop's La-Z-Boy recliner. I snag my favorite hoodie from high school and hike it over my head, as the night air has turned chilly.

The two men are still deep in conversation over some damn engine as I trot down the steps with two chilled long necks in my hand. Oren spots and signals no with his glance, but would never disrespect my dad. I swear the last of his beer ended up on my toes as he gracefully poured it under the table and then sipped my drink.

When I plop back down, I don't land in my chair, but in Oren's lap; he tenses up and I know it's because of my dad. Me, on the other hand don't give a shit, I pour the rest of the margarita into my glass and hand it over my shoulder to Oren and then begin sipping his beer.

The conversation goes on forever about hemis, transmissions, and corn fuel. None of it affects me and I have to bite my lip to hold back a few comments where I know for a fact they're wrong. It's from all the billing and parts I've seen float through the office. I let men be men and melt back into Oren.

After he realizes my father isn't going to behead him, he plays along with me, wrapping his safe arms around me. I'm not sure how I've fallen for him so fast, but all I do know is life wouldn't be the same without him. Countless nights tossing in my Macy's sheets, wondering if I'm just the next McSlut on his menu have proven me wrong. I'm at a ripe age and he's embraced every single awkwardly screwed up moment in my life from butt sex porn to ripping a world record fart in front of him. Oren never lets me live it down, but it's almost like he embraces me more for it.

"I'm going to bed, kids." Pops slams down his empty long neck on the glass top.

"I think we're going to stay here tonight, Old Man," I reply.

It wasn't planned or even thought out, but we've both drank enough along with my Pops that he needs supervision.

"You know where your bed is, Firecracker."

"Love you, too."

The screen door slams shut and he disappears into the house. My dad loves to talk and entertain the next person, but when he's at his limit, he'll let you know.

I swivel in Oren's lap until I'm face to face with him. "I bet there's more beer in the fridge. Want me to sneak a bottle out for you?"

"So damn witty all the time, Olivia." His fingers dig into my ass through my shorts.

"I'll mix you a drink," I offer.

"I think I know exactly where to stick my tongue to get the perfect drink."

My hips buck on cue with his words. "Oh really, where is that?"

Yard lights flip on, causing me to bound back into the harsh edge of the table. Moments later, Scout prances into the backyard, sending every single motion sensored light to high alert.

"Your dick out, Oren?"

"Nope, successful cock block," he hollers back over my shoulder.

"Perfect. I have more margaritas."

"Cock block excused." Oren pours himself a glass of the tarty liquid and then relaxes back. I remain calm, sipping from a beer.

"I can't stand it," Scout exclaims and then guzzles the pitcher. "I can't fucking stay there any longer and I don't want to go back to my apartment where Taylor and I have so many memories. I really thought..." She breaks off, not able to finish her thought, but I know exactly what she was going to say.

"I did, too." I cover the top of her hand with mine. "I did, too, Scout."

"It fucking sucks and if you break my sister's heart I'll..."

I stop her before she finishes.

"Scout, move in with me. It's dumb we have separate places."

"O, I'm not messing up what you have since you've never had any."

"By all means, thanks for pointing that out." I swat her shoulder, sloshing some beer on her. I feel Oren steady me a bit. "Move in with me."

"Do I have to share a bed with Pedro?"

"Depends," I respond. "If you're a good girl."

"Fuck off."

"Move in with me and split rent. I have a spare room. I can't promise if Pedro will pee on you or hump you, but you won't be alone."

"We've never lived together after college because I hump too much."

"Yeah, I won't argue that, Slut Wagon. You've worn down more mattresses than..."

"I get it. I get it." Scout waves me off. "I'm going back home."

"Should I help her?" Oren whispers in my ear. "I need to help her."

He has me on my feet and standing before Scout even pushes open the gate between our houses.

"She's fine, hun, unless we hear a loud thump then we know she ate shit on the flower pot, again."

"Are you sure?" he asks, worried about her safety.

"Go do your cop thing and flash lights and everything else. She's fine. It's not her first rodeo."

"Should she have thumped by now?"

I laugh and then reassuringly pat his chest. "Yes, by now she's in her bed and fast asleep. Trust me."

"Well, shit, my buzz has worn off."

"Mine too," I say with a giggle. "But I know where more alcohol is."

"Lead the way since we are staying the night."

I turn in his arms once again to face him. "Is it creepy we are staying here? You know, with my dad under the same roof and I'll admit it now I still have My Little Pony posters on the wall."

"I'm not driving and you're not driving, so I'm thinking My Little Ponies are making me horny right now."

"Wow, easy sell, there Hot Cop." I pat his chest as I make my way up the stairs to the back door. I'm walking up backwards and he's guiding each step I take. I don't second-guess his actions, only follow.

Once inside the house I take the lead, making the way to my bedroom on the bottom floor. A flight of steps down from the main section and we're in Olivia land. It's like an amusement park filled with my childhood memories my Pops never touched. He could have the ultimate man cave from cold beers to a pool tale, but he's chosen to leave all of my things in place. My cradle my mother rocked me in is now filled with my favorite stuffed animals from Rainbow Bright to Rainbow Dash the pony.

Oren's thankfully tangled in my lips and hair as I guide him back to my bedroom. There's one room off to the left of the stairs. It's hard to see among all my childhood and teenage memorabilia.

When the back of my calves hit the mattress and his hardened center collides into me, I know it's the time. Now or Never. Oren's ready, clearly with his bulging cock, which is typically on display during our make-out sessions and I'm in love.

I fall back easily onto the bed, lifting my tank over my head, and shimming down my shorts until I'm left only in lacy panties and a skimpy bra that reveals an escaped nipple.

"Your dad," he pants out, tugging down his own jeans.

"He's out. He pounded six beers and won't wake until seven in the morning." I slip my panties over the hump of my ass cheeks, spreading my legs as far as they can go until I feel Oren settled between them. The courage and boldness over taking my actions shocks me, but I know it's the need of wanting all of him.

"Are you sure, Olivia? I won't be able to stop, baby, once I start."

I press my palms to his broad shoulders. "Just don't break my heart, Oren."

"I'm not here to break your heart, Olivia." Oren's deep brown eyes peer up to me. "Trust me."

I only nod swallowing a lump in my throat.

Oren relaxes back down between my legs. I've felt his bare flesh before, but like this between my legs compares to nothing. *Okay, maybe meeting Mickey Mouse for the first time.*

Salty tears begin to roll down both of my cheeks as Oren's fingers slide in and out of me.

"Olivia, are you okay?"

I nod against his broad shoulder and let the tears fall from me. I'm unable to decipher if they're happy or sad tears. All I know is they're rolling off me like Niagara.

The ripping of a packet is the next sound I hear. Oren performs his signature move of clutching my wrist and dragging it to him. He wraps my fingers around his growing cock and then rolls my fingers over the condom striding down him. When I reach the base, I grasp it.

There's so much I've never done with him. Each time it's been Oren pleasing me and now with his want, need, and hunger in my hand, I feel powerful. I could reign over countries with this mass enveloped in my palm.

Oren dips his face low until his lips reach mine. He calms my nerves and reads my mind like so many times before. My hand slips from his base to the tip of his cock clothed in a condom and then finally roams to his ass cheek.

"You ready, Olivia?" His deep husky voice sends streams of ecstasy up my spine.

I nod into his flesh, unable to talk, paralyzed from all the emotions and feels sprinting through me. The tip of his cock nudges in me, and I groan feeling the same sensation as his fingers. His hips flex again, thrusting more of himself into me and it stings and with his final thrust, I bury my screams of pain and pleasure into the flesh of his shoulder.

"Olivia," he groans into the tender nape of my neck.

"It hurts," is the only reply I can muster up.

"Fuck," he growls out. "I never should've. I'm so sorry. I got greedy…"

"Shut up, Oren. I want you and I want this. I love you."

He makes another subtle move with his hips and it burns like a motherfucker. He repeats the slow motion over and over again until the friction is inviting just like his fingers when they swirl my sensitive bud. I focus on his smell and smile as he works his hips into me.

I dig my fingernails into his shoulder blades until his flesh comforts me. Each of his thrusts into me sends painful shockwaves throughout my body, but it's the flesh on flesh contact that keeps me grounded. His lips on my neck and hands wrapped around the back of my head steadying me.

I never ask him to stop or slow down. Each time he pounds into me it's an addictive time of pain I begin crave and even though he's on top, my hips begin subtly moving against his. I grind on him, feeling relief and also that same familiar feeling of desire pooling low in my belly.

"O…"

Oren never finishes his thought as the jagged tips of my nails sink into him and writhe harder and faster, finding my release. His grunts are deafening in my ear as he lets go, but never stops, slowly working his hips into me. It all feels like a dream until he speaks.

"Is this the ass of a pony?" He raises up a figure and between the light of my cellphone with social media alerts and the old school alarm clock on my nightstand, I spot the outline of Fluttershy's bright yellow tail.

"Yes, it's my pony." I squirm underneath Oren but don't let our connection separate.

"You never cease to amaze me, Olivia, never." He rises up. "Stay here. I'll be right back."

"Where are you going?"

My fucking panicked voice taunts me like no other. *I mean, really could I just scream was this the fuck and go drive thru? Because we don't supersize around here for anyone, not even hot cops.*

"I'm going to wash up and will be right back. Quit panicking."

Oren pads out of the room to the right and flips on the bathroom light switch. Must be his ninja detective skills that lead him in the right direction. The faucet runs for a bit and then the toilet flushes before I hear his size eleven feet making it back my way.

"Olivia," Oren whispers.

"Oren," I whisper right back.

"Jackass." He lets out a hearty laugh. "I'm going to clean you up. Thought you might be asleep."

"Your dick isn't that powerful," I taunt.

Oren's covering me head to toe in an instant, attacking me with his lips until I'm near coma status.

"What was that you were saying, Smartass?" he whispers into my ear.

I fumble a few times to produce a coherent thought until I give up and feel him snake down my body again. A warm damp rag is dragged carefully through my folds. He's gentle and caring all the while just winding my horny ass up once again. A quick dart of something cold and wet laps through me, causing me to scream and buck up into him.

"Olivia, this is my dessert." Both of his large palms splay across my pelvis as he sinks my hips back into the mattress.

His fingers were amazing and his Tony the Tiger magical, but that one dart of his tongue was out of this world. The sound of the rag being tossed aside brings me back to reality and then peeking up, I spot his wavy brown hair between my legs.

Without thought or care, I weave my hands into his hair and push him further into me. When his tongue makes contact again, I scream and buck. One of his hands races up to my mouth to cover it as his tongue begins working overtime inside me. He adds his fingers which are much gentler this time, letting his tongue do most of the work.

It only takes one swirl of his tongue, thrust of his finger, and buck of my hips to set me off once again. Oren presses his hand harder down into my screams and all I can do is buck up harder into his mouth. After each aftershock of pleasure subsides, my entire body collapses back into the mattress.

My brain thuds in my skull and then comes back to its senses when Oren weaves his way back up to me.

"Guess you just got the full meal deal." Sleep is heavy in my voice.

"No," he responds. "I wined and dined on the most exquisite feast ever."

I nuzzle into him, burrowing both of our naked bodies under the blanket. Our legs intertwine like old habit and I seal to him likes he's my oxygen.

"I love you, Olivia, I've loved since I laid eyes on you in your classroom. I've never believed in love at first sight until you. I just hope you don't break my heart."

I perch up on one elbow. "I'm not here to break your heart, Oren."

Chapter 16

Sexed

Sticky and extremely tangled bodies are all we seem to be these days. When he knocks on the door at three in the afternoon or one in the morning I'm dressed and ready for him and by dressed I mean naked under the sheets.

"When is Dr. Sex coming over?" Scout asks, rolling her eyes.

"He gets off at ten if all goes smooth on his shift."

"I'm taking my Ambien, Tylenol PM, Vicodin, and Valium cocktail now, so I don't have to hear the two of you sappy asses."

"We're not loud." I toss the throw pillow at her.

"Oren, stick it in my butt, please. Ride my ass until sunset," Scout mocks, dry humping the back of my couch.

"I've never said that."

"I know." She shrugs. "But be honest, the curious part of you wants to know how it feels rimming that asshole."

"Go search Tinder, Bitter Betty."

"Oh, I will and watch ample amounts of porn to drown you two out."

"You are so full of shit, Scout."

"Oh really, Miss Backbend off the bed while getting drilled and then performing the perfect back 360, landing it on your rug."

"You didn't knock." I stand to my feet ready to retreat, knowing the story she just recounted was spot on.

"I was getting my charger."

"Don't be a Jealous Jill."

"For fucksake school is out, enough with the graphemes and making me sound out shit."

"Oren or Dr. Sex will be here any minute, BTW."

"Oh, cute now your language of choice is texting acronyms."

"LOL."

"Hey, have you thought how you two are going to pound uglies while camping with your father? I mean, in the same trailer."

"We haven't discussed..."

"Oh wait, you lost your V card under his roof, so you're probably a seasoned expert at whorin' around."

The door opens to our apartment, alerting Pedro to a serial killer. Oh wait, it's my handsome hunky cop, but Pedro barks like he's about to make Mexico the fifty-first state in the US of A.

"I was so dumb to break my lease on my apartment." Scout stands and salutes Oren like any good soldier would before retreating to her bedroom.

"Hey." I stand and go to Oren.

"Hey you."

I kiss him quickly before guiding him to the kitchen and setting him down at the table and giving him his dinner. I know it's been a rough night for him since he only replied in one-word texts.

"Hungry?" I slide the chicken and rice his way while climbing into his lap.

"Starving." He kisses me in his fashion, deep and hungry. "Starving for you, Olivia."

"Aren't you romantic?"

"I need you now." He rises from the chair and carries me to my room, kicking the door shut behind us, but like any good cop he makes sure Pedro enters before kicking it shut.

He tosses me back on the bed and then begins stripping off his uniform. I'm dying to ask him to do a little dance for me, but the look in his eyes is not one to mess with. We've had full out sex only three times now and each times it's been gentle and with me on my back and him on top protecting me.

His broody eyes tell a different story tonight. He needs more and a lot more than I'm used to giving him.

"You okay, baby?" I ask and stare at him pulling down his boxers.

"I will be in a minute."

He makes quick work of peeling off my athletic shorts and ripping my tank from me. His lean and strong body covers mine, assaulting every single inch of it with his hot kisses and licks.

"Condom," I breathe out when the tip of him nudges my center.

"Not yet, O."

He slides down my body, leaving trails of kisses from my sternum all the way until he reaches my pelvic bone. My man knows me well.

"You spoil me." I intertwine my fingers in his hair, relishing the way his hot breath tickles me to the core.

Oren peers up at me and his gaze is as soft as his caress. He strokes a gentle growing fire inside me with his fingers. My hips meet each of his strokes while every other body part anticipates the sweep of his tongue on my center. My heart pounds wildly in my chest until I can feel it beating in my own ears.

His tongue takes the first sweep against my sensitive bud, causing me to buck further up into him. Oren's fingers pick up speed as does each flick of his tongue. A delicious shudder begins in my body as he continues swirling and working me over. Both of his hands grip into my ass cheeks, hoisting me up further into him and I'm shocked at the impact of his gentle grip. It sends me over the edge of passion, screaming out his name.

It takes moments for my breathing to settle down to an even beat. Oren works his way back up to me, lazily dragging his tongue up my bared flesh until he meets me face to face. I detect a flicker in his intense eyes before he punishes me with his lips, leaving a stinging bite on my bottom lip.

He rolls me over until I'm on top of him. Using my palms, I push up into a sitting position, confused and dazed from one of the best orgasms I've ever experienced.

"Your turn to be on top, Olivia." Oren grabs a condom from the top of my nightstand with one hand on my hip. I swallow tightly as I watch him use his teeth to tear the foil packet. He hands me the rubber to sheath him. It empowers me to know he wants this with me.

"I don't know what I'm doing." I look up to Oren through my hair cascading around my face. "You'll have to help me."

"I've got you, baby." Both of his hands grip into my hips gently lifting me, aligning me with him. His nearness is already overwhelming, putting all my senses on high alert. He's gentle as he eases me down on him.

He's huge, filling me all the way. I find it still hurts a bit, but once Oren begins his gentle movements, the bit of pain disappears, leaving behind breath-taking sensations.

"Move with my hands," he grits out.

His teeth sink into his bottom lips as he keeps eye contact with me.

"Holy shit. Stop." I plant both hands on his chest.

"Are you okay, baby?" He uses one hand to brush my hair away and cup my cheek.

"It's too much. I mean, I'm going to go in like three more seconds."

A devilish grin covers his face. "I know. I've thought about the look on your face while you were riding me all day at work. Just enjoy it. Take it slow."

His touch, voice, and smell kindles a stronger fire of feelings for him that I never knew possible between two people. I follow the rhythm of his one hand guiding me and lean into the other one clutching to my face. My nails dig into his chest with the movements I make.

A passionate flutter arises at the back of my neck and I know I'm so close. I don't want it to end, but the pain of being so close is deliciously taunting me.

"Go, Olivia, Go. I'll fall with you."

His deep voice coaxes my hips to move faster and land harder at his base. I struggle to keep quiet as the pleasure tears through my soul, leaving me sated. Oren grunts and then growls out my name as he pushes up from the bed deeper into me, letting go of his own release. I collapse down on him more in love than moments earlier.

"That'll do Hot Cop. That'll do." I pat his chest and smile when I feel his tender kiss on the top of my head.

"I bought us a tent," he says after we both have a chance to catch our breath.

"Oh yeah?"

"Figured it might get awkward in a trailer with your dad and I'm not sure if he's okay with us sleeping together."

"I'm not ten," I counter.

"It's a respect thing."

"Trust me. I'm sure my Old Man knows we've done the deed thanks to Scout."

"Speaking of Scout. How's she doing?"

I prop up on my elbow, admiring his gorgeous brown eyes for a second before speaking. "I'm not sure. I'm pretty sure she's already had rebound sex, but besides that, she's pretty quiet."

His stomach growls quite loudly, causing Pedro to fire off in a shower of barks. *That damn dog.*

"Get dressed and I'll go reheat your dinner," I say, slapping his chest and forcing myself to untangle from him. "Hey, why were you so moody when you came in?"

"Shitty day and I needed you." He winks at me while jumping into some jeans he's left here.

"Guess, you got what you wanted."

"And I'm not done tonight either."

His threat sends chills down my spine and they land right in my panties. "No shirt, please."

"Olivia, are you using me for my body?"

"Hell yes I am." I watch him zip up his zipper. "And leave them unbuttoned."

Oren envelopes me in a bear hug, showering slobbery kisses all over my face as he walks out into the living room until we're in the kitchen.

"Are you guys decent?" Scout hollers from her room.

"El Si," I shout right back, popping Oren's dinner into the microwave for a few seconds.

"God, Olivia, you're a screamer." Scout takes up a seat at the small oak dining room table.

"No, I'm not. It's just Oren is a sex god."

"Ugh, shut up about sex and being in love already," she replies while studying her phone. "So, are you working tomorrow?"

"Yeah," I reply, setting Oren's plate in front of him. "Dad has a new guy coming in."

"Holy shit," Scout exclaims.

"I know. Surprised me too, but I guess he's finally figuring out I'm not going to ever be a mechanic and he needs help."

"You'd be sexy as hell covered in grease," Oren says around a bite of food.

"God, you two are disgusting." Scout rolls her eyes.

"Now you know how it feels, but anyway, planning on leaving right after work. Dad's pulling the trailer and we're riding with him and before you ask, Oren bought a tent for us."

"That poor tent; there will be baby batter everywhere," Scout chimes.

"You jealous," I taunt and by her reaction she's genuinely surprised by my comment. I'm sure she expected me to be grossed out. Between her and Oren, they've brought out my inner wildcat.

"You'll be strumming your clit-tar in your parent's camper."

HJ Bellus

Chapter 17

Exposed Beaver

"He's so fucking hot," I sip on my spiked iced tea and stare at the shirtless Oren setting up our tent.

His lean torso glistens with his sweat beads as he pounds the stakes into the ground. His deep V is exposed, giving me all sorts of dirty thoughts like dragging my tongue along the outline of it.

"You're practically dry humping the air, O." Scout nudges me in the arm.

"Well, do you blame me?" I point to Oren.

"No, but I kind of hate you if I'm being honest. He's the perfect catch."

"That he is and he's all mine."

I strut over to Oren and hand him my ice-cold tea.

"Thanks, babe. Like our castle?"

"Love it."

"I can't wait to break it in tonight." Oren bends down, placing a kiss on my lips and then getting right back to work.

I join Scout and her mother, who are relaxed back in loungers sipping on their own cocktails.

"This is my favorite part, girls." We both turn to her. "Watching the men do all the work."

I pull my tank top off and lay in the sun, soaking in some rays.

"Where did your dad find Diesel?" Scout asks.

Between the warmth of the sun on my olive skin and the buzz from my drink, I have to ask Scout to repeat her question.

"Oh shit, I don't know, why?"

"Just curious."

"He seems like a nice guy. Met him before we took off. A little hard to get past his name though."

I doze back off, enjoying the sound of the mountains and the men working. I'm not sure how long I sleep before Oren wakes me.

"Want to go fishing, Sleeping Beauty?"

"Yeah," I wipe the sleep from my eyes.

"Your dad has your hot pink My Little Pony pole ready." Oren doesn't contain his amusement.

"Listen here, Mister, that pole is badass."

"It's something." He kisses my forehead as I stand up and steady myself to put back on my tank.

"No." He tosses it back in the chair. "Want a ride?"

"Oh, I want a ride, trust me."

"That's for later." He turns his back to me.

With gusto, I lace my arms around his neck and then jump up. Oren catches each of my ankles, helping me hook them around his midsection.

"I likey smashed boobies in my back."

"Giddy-up, Cowboy."

He begins trotting down to the stream where we always fish. Dad's brought me here since I could walk. My mom never fished, but loved watching and cooking them up for us.

"I don't know what I'd do without you in my life, Olivia."

"What brings that up?" I lay my head on his shoulder and nibble at his ear.

"I just don't. I love this and you. Camping, your dad, friends, and your boobies smashed in my back."

"I love this too. It's something I never thought I'd get to experience."

We reach the stream, Dad and his cooler coming into view. He has the chairs set up and two ice-cold beers set on top of the cooler.

"Looks like Pops is trying to turn you into a beer man."

"Oh, Olivia, I can't stomach another one."

"Just tell him you want a cocktail."

"And lose all my manhood," he says, setting me down on my feet and then turning to me, beating on his chest. "I am man. I must drink beer and catch fish with my bare hands."

"Hey kids." Dad waves at us and holds up a beer for Oren. "I have your pole ready, Firecracker, and your spot saved."

"Your spot saved?" Orren asks, taking the beer like a champ.

"It's my lucky spot with my kickass pole." I crawl over the cooler and Oren's chair until I find my favorite rock I always fish from.

I cast my line out and then sit down, dipping my toes in the cool water and when I look over to Oren he's snapping a pic of me with his phone.

"What are you doing?" I ask.

"Taking a picture of the gorgeous scenery."

I beam back at him. "You better get your fish on unless you want to be whipped by me."

"You don't stand a chance, Oren, she out fishes anyone. Might as well enjoy the river and drink beer."

"Yeah, babe, drink up."

Oren scoops up a handful of water, splashing me with it, and then turns his hat on backwards.

"It's on."

Dad and Oren fall into easy conversation about cars and different engines. When Dad asks him how he got involved in cars, he replies his granddad. I realize it's the first time I've ever heard him really talk about his family. His granddad was his idol.

The sun begins to set low behind the outline of the mountains.

"Got another one." I yank up on the pole, snagging the fish, and begin reeling it in. "Bam bitches, suck it hoes! That's six for me and how many for you boys?"

I stand on the rock with my hand on my hip and a gorgeous trout dangling from my pole.

"Told you, son, we didn't stand a chance." Dad stands up, grabbing the cooler. "I'll meet you kids back up at camp."

I begin a silly victory dance on top of my rock.

"Get your cute ass over here."

I unhook my fish and put it on the line in the water with the rest of our catch.

"These will be so yummy for dinner tonight." I tip-toe through the water until I reach him.

Oren wastes no time dragging me down into him and wrapping me up.

"I think I'm starting to develop a taste for beer."

"You are drunk." I take his hat off and ruffle his hair.

"You caught all the damn fish so I had to drink and be a man."

"I love you, baby." I brush my lips against his and feel him stand to attention.

"Thank you for inviting me here. I never did anything like this as a kid."

"I'm so happy you came." I kiss him again with more vigor leaning into him, smashing those boobies into his chest like he loves. In slow motion, the chair leans back and with Oren lit we both go with the flow until we're both in the water and floating down the stream.

"Your phone!"

"It's on the shore."

I cling to him for dear life until we hit a swimming hole where there's no current.

"I used to swim as a kid."

I feel Oren drag my shorts down along with panties. He tosses both up onto a large rock sticking out of the water. He lets go of me, then I see his shorts fly up onto the rock.

"Come here." He holds out a hand.

"Are you standing?"

"On all three legs." He shoots me a cheesy smile.

I wrap my arms around his neck and then legs around his waist and he wasn't shitting me about having three legs. The tip of him bobs at my entrance, causing me to close my eyes and moan.

"We don't have protection."

"I won't let go inside you."

"What about..."

He interrupts with his voice and a thrust of his hips. "Do you trust me, Olivia?"

I don't answer but instead sink down until he's in me. The pain lasts for a second until he begins working in and out of me.

"Shhhh, baby. Your dad and friends are right up over those bushes."

"Fuck, Oren." I clutch around his neck, hanging on for dear life and enjoying each of his thrusts. I try muffling my moans in his neck, but end up sputtering on water splashing up in my face.

My body reacts to each one of his movements. He makes me feel every single thing imaginable. I pull back a bit, clutching to his face and burying my screams in him. I attack his mouth as my belly tightens with unbearable pleasure. I bite down on his bottom lip and feel him freeze right when I was ready to let go.

"Oren, why did you stop?" I try to kiss his lifeless lips.

"Bear," he mumbles into my lips.

"Uh?" I pull back to look at his face and notice his gaze over my shoulder.

A fucking black bear is standing in the water right across the stream from us. We watch in silence as he picks up Oren's chair that's stuck in the rocks and then sends it flying. He dips his head in the water and pulls out a fish.

"The fucker has my fish," I yell.

Oren slaps his hand over my mouth. "Olivia, shut the hell up. He's going to be eating us next."

I bite at Oren's hand until he removes it. "Those are my damn fish."

"Be quiet."

"Dad," I scream. "Bear."

"Jesus Christ, Olivia. My dick is hanging out and a bear is about to eat us. Can you please shut up?"

I pick up a rock and toss it at the bear, trying to spook him away. I nearly hit him. I step up out of the water, getting my footing on a sandy bar, and sling another rocket in the asshole's direction.

Scout comes busting through the bushes and then screams like her hair is on fire. I'm pretty sure Scout literally scared the shit out of the bear as he took a big dump and then ran off away from our camp.

"Jesus fuck, Olivia nothing like sending me right into a trap."

"He was eating my fish."

"You and your dumb fish." Scout places a hand on her hip and yells a little louder across the stream. "Speaking of fish, your vagina is hanging out."

I sink back down into the swimming hole right when my dad and the rest join the circus act known as Olivia. I can't hear Scout, but can see her relaying the whole story using her hands. I'm just hoping she leaves out the exposed beaver part.

I turn to Oren, who passes me my shorts and panties under the water.

"You're dressed, right?"

"Damn straight and sober as a nun. I was ready to run."

"You wuss." I laugh and wiggle into my shorts.

"Hey, it's survival. I just have to be the fastest one to live."

"You jerk!" I jump back up into his arms. "You are quite the scaredy cat not in your uniform."

"It was a bear for Christ sake and little ol' you were just chucking rocks at it so he wouldn't eat your fish." Oren begins walking us back to the shore and I swear he's still shaking.

"Make me a stiff one." Oren plops down in one of the loungers and I can't help but bust up.

"Your damn daughter is crazy," he tells my dad.

Dad chuckles before he responds, "The girls likes to fish."

I dump a fair share of vodka into the red plastic cup, fill the rest of it up with sweet tea, and squeeze lemon in it before handing it to Oren.

"What were you guys doing across the stream?" Scout asks with a smirk on her face.

"Swimming," I reply.

"Just swimming," she counters.

Oren chokes on his drink.

"Yes, just swimming, asshole," I grit out.

Chapter 18

Did You Hear That?

Farkle around the campfire with everyone toasted and having a ball. I'm curled up in Oren's lap snuggled in to keep warm. Once the sun goes down in the mountains, it gets right down titty cold.

"I'm ready for s'mores," Scout declares and throws her dice on the table.

"Just because you are losing, loser," I taunt.

"Cum guzzler," she growls.

"Girls, enough," her mother scolds.

"She's not one of those, sir," Oren says to my dad.

The situation went from relaxing to beyond awkward.

"I'll help Scout." I bounce up from Oren's lap and head for the trailer.

"What in the hell is your problem?" I ask, slamming the door.

"I miss Taylor." Scout busts out into tears. "I loved him."

"I know." I wrap her up in a hug and let her cry. Scout always masks everything, rarely letting her true feelings show and just relies on her witty and smartass humor to get her through life.

"His new girl is pregnant."

"Oh shit. How do you know?"

"I stalk her Facebook. She's like five months pregnant, O."

"I'm so sorry, honey." I pet her hair and let my best friend's tear fall in my lap. There's not much you can say in a situation like this to make her situation any better.

"Want to go do s'mores?" I ask her.

"No, I'm just going to go to bed." She sits up and wipes the last of the tears away from her welted eyes.

"C'mon, it's tradition."

"We'll be here three more damn nights."

I snag her nipple between my two fingers. "I'll twist if you don't get your ass out there with your best friend and make s'mores."

"You wouldn't."

"I would." I apply a bit of pressure before she finally gives in.

Scout and I snuggle up in a lounger together, roasting marshmallows and becoming a sticky mess while the Farkle game comes to an end. Oren pours himself another drink and joins. Scout tries to stand up, but I force her back down in the chair.

"You girls are doing it all wrong," Oren says, sipping on his drink.

"Excuse me?"

"Here, put a marshmallow on." He holds out his poker and then surveys the fire before he decides on a place. "See, the secret to s'mores is melting your chocolate."

He takes a graham cracker, placing a chocolate square on it and setting it on a rock near the fire. It only takes him moments to have one ready.

"Here, Scout, see what you think?"

I watch her devour the s'more.

"Best ever," she says, closing her eyes and chewing.

I glance back to the fire and notice mine on fire. "Shit."

I begin whipping it wildly into the air.

"God dammit, Olivia, I've told you since you were a toddler not to do that."

I turn to my dad, who has a burnt and smooshed marshmallow in the bill of his hat.

"Dad, I'm sorry." I cover my mouth to mask my giggles. "I just react."

"Take the stick away from her, Oren," Dad instructs and it makes me laugh even harder being treated like a four year old.

"See this scar on my neck." My dad points to it. "A flying, flaming marshmallow sent into launch by this shit."

Oren takes my stick away and hands me a s'more while fighting to hide his amusement. The rest of the group huddles around the fire sharing stories from our past. I stay huddled to Scout and prop my leg up on Oren who's settled onto a log next to me.

"Remember the time Scout put the cat in the dryer?" Her dad lets out a hearty howl at the memory.

"I do. My dad whipped my ass for it and I didn't even do it."

"You got the stool for me to push start, so you were an accomplice."

"You two were hell on wheels," Scout's mom adds.

"Feel sorry for the future men in your life." Dad elbows Oren and squeezes Scout in a hug.

"You'll find your Mr. Right." I hug her tight.

Oren continues to make s'mores and eats his fair share of them. The dab of smeared chocolate at the corner of his lip tempts me.

"Shots," Scouts yells, jumping to her feet. "We need damn shots."

She grabs the bottle of vodka and jar of pickles and begins pouring a round of shots.

"Why?" I groan, joining her at the picnic table.

"Because all good stories start with shots." She hands me my two cups. "Oren."

"What is this?" He wrinkles his nose.

"Pickle juice you chase the vodka with," I reply.

Scout holds her cup up and we both follow. I peeked in before raising and it's definitely equivalent to two shots.

She toasts. "To friends, orgasms, really good sex, and to my vibrator."

It's downright loveable when Oren looks at me for the okay to cheers to Scout's vibrator. I give him the nod and then we shoot the vodka followed by the pickle juice.

"My turn." I pour the shot, being careful not to pour so much vodka in the damn plastic cups and then line up the pickle juice.

Everyone grabs their cups and raise them up under the moon. "To love, friendship, and summer nights."

Oren slaps my ass as he downs the shots. I squeal and then take mine. I lose track of the toasting, shots, and other drinks. All three of us howl at the moon and each other's jokes. Oren tells Scout the fart story and I elbow the shit out of him.

"Bedtime before someone falls in the fire," Oren stands and clearly is the most sober out of all of us.

"Yes, Officer," Scout replies.

"He's my sexy Occifer."

"Move it, girls. You've howled at the moon long enough tonight."

"Hey Occifer are you going to do an anal cavity search on my O tonight?"

"Whatsss that?" All of my words slur together.

"His hand in a rubber glub up your anus."

"Goes to bed," I order her, waving my Solo cup in the direction of her parents' trailer but somehow pour most of the vodka into the fire. And talk about holy Jesus of fireball.

"That's how they make Fireball," Scout yells.

"I knows."

"Bed now," Oren growls.

His speech is very clear and demanding.

"Or what?" Scout counters.

"You's gonna have to handcuff us, Occifer schemxy?"

In one swoop, he has me over his shoulder, and dragging Scout by the wrist until we reach her parents' trailer doors. He opens the door and shoves her in.

"Nice police skills," I say upside down.

"Not even my police skills can handle the two of you together."

"I'm gonna puke dangling like this."

Oren slides me back down his chest.

"Wrap your legs around my middle."

"I want marshmallows. Can we roast more?"

"No."

"Chips. Let's eat chips."

"No."

"Cake. Let's eat cake."

"No, we're going to bed, baby."

"I want a hotdog."

"Want an elephant?"

I spring up from resting on his shoulder. "Yes, I want an elephant."

His deep laugh vibrates against my chest. "You're so wasted, Olivia."

"I can see twos of you right now."

"I bet you can, sweetie."

"It's my palace," I squeal.

I hear the zipper going down and then Oren sets me on the ground.

"Stay in here," he says in a harsh voice.

"Where are you going?"

"I'm going to drown out the fire. Olivia, please stay in the tent."

"Don't get eaten by a bear." I laugh at my own joke. Oren doesn't laugh, but goes for the fire.

He has battery-operated lanterns hung in the tent and our sleeping bags laid out. I strip like it's my day job by trade and snuggle down in his over-sized one. Even sober, I hope he didn't think I was sleeping in my own bag.

"Olivia."

"Yes, big daddy."

"Where in the hell are you?"

I pop up from under the warmth of the top layer of sleeping bag. "Here."

Both of my boobs flop out as I sit up.

"That's mine."

"Come join me, grumpy pants."

Oren peels his pants off, then hoodie.

"Boxers."

"Olivia."

"Boxers, now. Body heat so we don't freeze."

Oren takes a few steps towards me and I'm up to tug on them, freeing him.

"What do we have here?" I smile up at him, going to my knees.

It seems he's more than excited to jump in the sleeping bag with me. I wrap my hand around the base of him and squeeze until I hear him groan.

"Help me." I stare into his eyes.

Oren places his hand over the top of mine and begins guiding it from the base of him to the tip, first slow then faster and slowing it back down. He adjusts the grip of his hand as we change speeds.

"Olivia," he grunts out. "You are too drunk to be doing this."

"I know exactly what I'm doing." And that's when my liquid courage kicks in.

I kiss the tip of his shaft first, then begin swirling my tongue around it before I take him whole into my mouth. Oren's deep satisfying groan fuels my desire to please him like he's done to me with his mouth.

I move faster, taking him deeper and then slowing down just like he did. I pop my mouth off his cock and then catch it between my teeth and suck harder than ever with my hand guiding the way. I feel him grow inside my mouth as he tries to push me away, but I hold onto his thigh, not letting go of him.

"O...O...Olivia," he grunts as he releases in my mouth.

Oren collapses to his knees, kissing my nose then cheeks, and then staring into my eyes.

"That was fucking mind blowing."

"I love you even when I'm drunk." I whisper on his lips.

"You are my everything, O."

He guides me back down into the sleeping bag and curls me back into his chest.

"Easy clean up with blow jobs, eh."

His deep chuckles are soothing as I'm already on the brink of sleep.

"Yes, they are."

Oren begins talking about work, my eyelids grow heavy, and I try to focus as long as I can, but soon lose the battle, falling fast asleep.

"I'm so fucking thirsty," I grumble as I tumble out of the tent into the glaring sunshine. My stomach heaves and the dry gags begin. "Water. I need water."

"See you two had a little too much fun last night." Dad's perched at the picnic table with his cup of coffee sipping on it.

Empty vodka and beer bottles are scattered everywhere. *I'm going to die.*

"You look like fuck." I turn to the side to see Scout huddled in an opening surrounded by bushes with a couple gallons of water and a bottle of ibuprofen.

"Water," I growl like a rabid animal. "I need water."

I fall to the soft dirt and grab a jug, downing it.

"I fucking hate you. No more shots." I wipe the water droplets from my mouth.

"I'm going to die, O, I don't even remember getting back to the trailer."

"Oren led you by the wrist like a fucking toddler." I laugh my ass off remembering that part.

She slaps both of her hands over her mouth. "Oh my God, that's so embarrassing."

"You girls want eggs?" I hear Scout's mom holler.

"I can't eat."

"You have to, O. It will help." Scout cups her hands around her mouth. "Yeah, Ma! Over easy, extra grease and heavy on the hot sauce."

"I swallowed baby batter last night."

I wait for her reaction and it never comes. She only waves and I turn to see Oren standing behind me and I don't even feel embarrassed or a flush creep up my spine. It may be the hangover or the fact my level butt puckering embarrassments have expired.

Chapter 19

Cherry Pie

"Don't tell me how to drive."

"You're speeding and haven't used your damn signal one damn time."

"I'll pull over. Want me to fucking pull over?"

"No, superstar, by all means drive it like you stole it so we make it to the damn community picnic on time."

A red light comes into view and I slam on the brakes, sending Oren sailing a bit forward; the seatbelt locks and I giggle.

"Again, would you like to drive, Officer?"

"Nope, sexy teacher." He reaches over and kisses the side of my head. "Just slow down."

"Don't tell me how to drive," I grit out with a fake smile.

"So, your dad sponsors this?"

"He's one of the main businesses that does. It's an annual thing."

"Barbecue, fireworks, beer, you know all the typical shit for the Fourth of July."

"And your tiny red shorts and tight-ass flag tank top?"

"That's tradition, too; Scout and I always get them at Old Navy."

"Olivia, slow down."

"Oren, do not tell me how to fucking drive," I yell each word.

When drive leaves my mouth the back of the car is lit up with red and blue lights and then the lovely sound of a cop's siren goes off.

"Shit." I hit the steering wheel with my hand and look over to Oren, who crosses his arms over his chest and sends me a sideways look. "Shut up, Oren, just shut up."

"I didn't say a word, Jeff Gordon."

I'd never admit it to him, but every single part of my body shivers in nerves, my heart races out of control, and I begin panicking. This will be my fourth speeding ticket and my father will flip his freakin' lid. Oh, that's right, I'm still on daddy's insurance

"What's the rush?" I look over to an officer leaning in the window. He looks familiar, but I can't quite place him.

"Sorry, Officer, didn't realize I was speeding."

"You were going seventy in a marked fifty-five."

"Oh really, that fast?" I feign as much innocence as humanly possible.

Oren clears his throat, then the officer ducks his head a bit more to see him.

"Sup, man?" the officer chirps out.

"Just going to the community shin-dig."

"Beats working, eh? Miss patrolling with ya, man."

And freakin' bingo, I place his face. It's Oren's old partner, which between the two of them quickly built a reputation around town of being hard asses. Tommy has even given his own grandma a speeding ticket. I have no chance of getting out of this one.

He quickly looks back to me and in his best police officer voice. You know the one meant to scare the shit out of you and put the fear of God in you, so you never speed again? Clearly has never worked out in my case.

"License, registration, and insurance."

I pluck my license from my wallet and then reach over to the glove box to get the registration and insurance. I make sure to let my boobs bounce on Oren's knee just trying to convince tough cop to get me out of this. I wiggle my way deeper into the glove box to grab the registration. Letting my girls massage the top of his knee.

"Got an itch?" Oren asks when I sit up.

I'm desperate. I even give him the puppy dog eyes, but he sits there with his arms crossed over his chest.

"I'll be right back, ma'am. Let me go run these."

Once the officer is in his car and out of earshot, I turn to Oren. "Help me. My dad is going to kill me."

"I told you to slow your ass down."

"Blah, blah, blah...that's old news. Please?" I whine.

"I hope you get a ticket. I'd slap you with one."

"Butthole." I whap his shoulder.

A passing car lays on their horn as they pass and of course it's fucking Scout who will beat me to the park, tell my dad about the ticket and get Ruby's famous cherry pie.

"Stupid cops," I mumble.

"Alright, ma'am, you'll need to have this paid by the end of the month. I'm citing you for speeding. The fine is one hundred ninety dollars and if you'd like to contest here's the information for that." He points to each section of the ticket.

"Yeah, I'm going to really protest it with Mr. Hardass sitting here next to me."

"Just doing my job."

"Happy Fourth of July," I reply, trying to be polite.

"See ya buddy." He waves to Oren.

"Take care, man and stay safe tonight." Waves.

It's the first time he's uncrossed his arms.

"You are mean," I blurt out, turning to him.

"You do know that's the guy who's ticketed his own grandma and kindergarten teacher. It didn't matter if I was sitting here and..."

"Shut-it, I know you said to slow down, but I even rubbed my boobies on your kneecaps and you didn't say one word to help me out."

I throw the papers back into the glove box.

"Yes, I did, Olivia."

"Oh, really?"

"I told you to slow your ass down."

"That was before..." And then the lightbulb goes off. "You knew he was patrolling out here, didn't you?"

"Like I said, I told you to slow down."

"My whole life is ruined. Scout's told my dad by now and snagged Ruby's famous cherry pie. She only brings one each year and now I won't get a piece, not even a morsel."

Oren laughs. The asshole has the courage to laugh.

"It's not funny. My life is ruined and I'm not driving." I throw the keys at his chest.

"C'mon, Olivia, don't you think you're being a bit over dramatic."

"No, I'm a girl who likes the best cherry pie on Earth on the Fourth of July and you ruined that."

The asshole only laughs harder and louder at me.

"I'm not driving." I climb over into his lap and face him, my arms crossed.

"You better get your ass over in that seat and drive before he comes back around and tickets you again."

"No."

"My, my, Olivia, I do believe I'm seeing your first fit."

"Yep. And you know what, since I don't get any pie then I'll have my dessert here."

I drag my tank over my head and toss it in the driver's seat, leaving me in my bikini top.

"Olivia."

"Are you warning me again, Officer?"

"You're going to get us in trouble, missy."

"I don't care. I wanted pie and got a ticket."

It only takes moments for Oren's hands to grip on my ass, tugging me closer to him.

"You think you need something, Olivia?"

I nod my head, rubbing our noses together, and then grind my hips into him. Oren sneaks his fingers down the front of my shorts.

"Mmmm. I'm still mad at you for not getting me out of that ticket."

"Maybe this will help you forgive me?"

He winds his hand into my hair and fists a clump of it, tugging my head back. His lips kiss the flesh on my exposed neck. I flex my hips into his hand, splaying across my tender parts, just begging him to enter me.

"Oren," I whimper out, moving my hips faster.

His teeth bite down on my skin and that's when he enters me with two fingers while his thumb swirls my sensitive bud. Holy shit, I had no idea how amped up I was. My hips move faster and with each push I move closer to the O.

"Next time I tell you to slow down you better listen." Oren's hand freezes inside of me.

"Oren, don't stop."

"Did you hear me?"

I move my hips in a panic, not wanting to lose any of the built-up sensation.

"Yes and yes Officer, I'll never speed again. Please, Oren."

I don't even think I was this whiny when begging for a My Little Pony as a kid. I need him and I need this damn O since I won't be getting any damn pie. Oren begins playing me again like a fine-tuned instrument. The need and want build right back up in me and it only takes seconds for it to burst inside of me.

His name rolls of my tongue in a shout as I ride out the O until my body has soaked up every single delicious sensation of it.

Cop lights flash as the officer passes us again.

"I don't even care if I get another ticket right now."

Oren's deep chuckle tickles my neck. "C'mon, I'll drive.

We untangle our bodies, then Oren rounds the car and drives the rest of the way to Oskar Lakes. I melt back into the seat, watching him from the corner of my eye, and still find myself in shock that he's mine. He's so damn sexy in his button up shirt. He always rolls his sleeves up to his elbows.

"What are you thinking about?" he asks me as he turns into the park.

"That I can't believe a man as sexy as you likes me."

"I'm one lucky man. That's all I can say. Love you, Olivia."

"Love you, too. Are you ready for an epic Fourth of July barbecue minus cherry pie?"

He gets out of the car, rounds it quickly, opens my door, and pulls me from the car. "The Fourth is my favorite holiday and I wouldn't want to be anywhere else, Olivia, cherry pie or not."

He whirls me around in his arms and positions his phone to take a selfie. Standing in his arms, I feel beautiful. Every inch of my skin glows. He takes a couple.

"Hey selfie-whore one more," I tell him.

He aims the camera at us again. I turn and kiss his cheek before he snaps it and freezes. We take several more until we are lip locked and he's still snapping away.

"Olivia." Scout's mom runs up to us out of breath. "Did you pick up the hotdog buns?"

"Oh shit. Just kidding. Yeah, we got them."

"Where do they need to go?" Oren asks. "I'll grab them."

Scout's mom gives Oren the instructions and they fade into the masses. I can see Oren for a while because of the towering stack of buns he's packing and the poor man has three more trips.

"Here, baby." I grab my sleeping dog and put on his cute Fourth of July outfit and then harness him and grab his doggy diaper bag.

Dad always has a tent sent up for us to find shade and relax. Several vendors are set up with drinks and sweet treats. Dad and a couple other businesses supply a free meal to the community. It's nothing fancy, just hotdogs and burgers, but Dad loves doing it. I swear he lives for this damn event.

"Olivia." I turn to see him in his apron flipping burgers.

"Hey Pops." I wrap him in a big hug.

"So, did Oren get you out of a ticket?"

"It's a long story."

Dad chuckles. "Our tent is set up over there."

"Okay, let Oren know too please."

And just like every single year, Dad has tables and chairs set up under the tent with coolers stocked with ice-cold drinks.

"Hey Diesel."

"Olivia."

He's a man of very few words, but working his ass for Dad. He may love cars as much or more than Dad. Diesel's a good-looking guy too with dark hair and blue eyes. Tattoos cover both of his arms. He definitely has the bad boy appeal.

Arms wrap around the back of me and I know it's Oren from the scent of his cologne.

"God, you look so sexy in those damn shorts."

"Thanks, baby."

"This place is crazy. I swear I ran into half your students."

"Oh yeah, the whole town comes out for it. Can you tie Pedro to something? The little bastard will take off if you don't."

"Got it."

"I'm going to get our stuff settled," I say while shaking my butt to a Lady Gaga song blaring from the stage.

Oren ties the end of Pedro's cord to one of the legs on the tent, but makes sure it's long enough so he can jump up in his lap. I watch Oren snag a beer from the cooler and then settle into one of the chairs.

"Hey, I'm Oren." He extends his hand to Diesel.

"Diesel."

I stare at the two, comparing them and realizing they couldn't be any different. Bad boy and Mr. All-American.

"Hey, you have that Shelby, right?" Diesel asks.

I swear to God Oren puffs his chest out, nods his head, and then takes a long pull from his beer.

"I am going to puke." I turn to see Scout walking up to me. "I am either going to puke or shit myself."

Both men turn around and for the first time in the history of Scout, she blushes with embarrassment and tries to play it off.

"Too much pie?" Oren asks. "I had to hear about it the whole damn drive."

Both men go back to conversing.

"You could've given me a signal, bitch," Scout hisses.

"Oh because I knew what you were going to say and anyhow, when do you ever give a shit about what you say?"

"Olivia, don't say shit. I really think my butthole is going to prolapse. I gobbled down that whole fucker before you got here," she whispers.

"Serves you right!"

"It's worth it. You won last year and I got you back. No cherry pie for you."

Scout lays on a blanket, clutching her belly, and moaning every so often. The rest of us eat and enjoy each other's company. Dad finally joins us smelling like a greasy burger. I'm in awe how well everyone is getting along. Oren and I have taken a few walks around the lake with Pedro and even ran into Kane. He dragged me out to the dance floor and made me do the damn chicken dance with him, which nearly gave me a heat stroke.

So, we're all back under the tent cooling off and waiting for the night sky to settle for the fireworks.

"Officer O'Brien." A new voice catches all of our attention. "Sorry to interrupt you."

"No problem." Oren stands up.

"Do you remember me?"

"I do. Ruby right?" He nods his head. "How are you feeling?"

"Healing quite nicely. You know that wreck was something awful and you were so nice to me, keeping me calm."

"No worries."

"Leo, get over here." Ruby turns and yells, startling all of us.

Her little husband comes scurrying up carrying a box. Holy shit, it can't be! Oh my hell, he's carrying a pie.

"I'm known around these parts for my pies, especially the cherry one. I'd like to give one to you for being such a great officer."

I leap from my chair to dry hump Oren's leg.

"That's awful kind of you. My girlfriend here is quite obsessed with your cherry pie."

That just sounded totally wrong.

"Oh yes, Miss Olivia." Ruby smiles proudly.

As soon as Ruby and Leo leave, I leap up into Oren's arm.

"Oh my God, I love you. I love you."

Then I hop down, snag the pie, and grab a fork.

"Olivia, please." Scout tries to use her pathetic puppy dog eyes on me.

"Not a chance, whore."

I slide the fork through the perfect flaky crust oozing right down into the filling. When the first taste hits my lips, I moan like I've never moaned before, closing my eyes and all.

I swallow the first bite and then announce, "It's so damn good. I just had an orgasm in my mouth."

Dad turns to Diesel. "Told you they're a bunch of freaks."

Oren straddles the picnic table facing me, pulling my legs up onto his. "Do I get to taste this cherry pie?"

I nod, scooping him up a big tasty bite and then feed it to him.

"You also get my cherry pie later tonight too, baby."

Oren clutches the back of my neck, dragging me to him. His lips taste like cherry and I devour them as the first set of fireworks go off in the night sky.

The Big O

Chapter 20

Surprise!

I have no idea where the summer has vanished. Time has flown by and I'm not ready for my freedom to be gone. Actually, I do know where my time has been spent; I've been busy sucking dick and tangled in life altering sex with my Hot Cop.

Oren worked late last night and ended up going to his apartment. It's pathetic that my own lady bits miss him that much. I mean, it was just one day and sleep without him. He's going back in this morning. I guess he's lead detective on some case and nuts deep in work. It's what he loves.

I strip down naked and find my longest jacket that I own in my closet. I'm going to pay my man a visit. I mean a quickie is better than nothing, right?

"Why in the hell do you have a winter coat on in August?" Scout asks from the couch. "Oh God, Oh Jesus take the wheel. Don't answer that question. You're a total slut biscuit."

"I miss him, Scout." I plop down opposite from her.

"Please keep your legs shut. I don't need a beaver shot this early in the morning."

I waggle my eyebrows at her. "You know you love me, but seriously how bad is that; I miss just being away from him one night."

"You've got it bad. Have you thought about moving in together?"

"I've thought about it, but haven't asked him." I pick at a loose thread on my coat. "I think he likes staying here."

"If he moves in here then I call dibs on his apartment. Fucking ear muffs don't even begin to muffle the noise you two rabbits make."

"You think you're ready to be on your own?"

Scout nods.

I know when she's quiet that something is really up. "Spill."

"What?" She squeals like a little child who's been caught with their hand in the cookie jar.

"Who is he?" I push.

"I'm not saying only because I don't want to jinx it."

"Is it serious?"

"No, he doesn't even know I'm crushing on him."

"Tell me," I whine. "I'm your best friend."

"No."

"Please."

"Nope."

"I'll flash my kitty right now if you don't."

"Fine, it's Pedro."

"You asshat. You're not going to give it up, are you?"

"It's probably just a silly crush, you know. I'm trying to do things differently since my track record is pathetic."

"If it becomes more serious or even a thing, you better tell me first."

"Deal." Scout nods.

"Shit, I've got to get going. Oren has to go back in at nine."

"Have fun, whoreface."

"Oh I will. It's a good ride."

"Gross. Shut it."

I can't help but drive with a goofy grin on my face. I'm so happy for Scout and super impressed she's going about dating differently. I just wonder who the mystery man is. The other reason for my smile is Oren. I can't wait to see his face when I drop this coat.

The fucker is hot,. I have the AC blasting as I drive. I spot his cars in his parking spot. I dig the key he gave me from my purse, squirt on his favorite perfume, and add some sexy red lipstick.

I shake my head in disbelief of the vixen Oren has brought out in me. Then I feel a pang of anxiety form deep in my tummy. I don't want to go back to work since that just means less time with him. Our schedules will be so different.

I bound from the car, leaping up his stairs in my heels, and then turn the key as quiet as can be. My luck he'll probably pull a pistol on me. Probably not the smartest thing to do...sneak into a cop's house. I second-guess my plan before turning the doorknob.

When I step in, I hear his shower running and Oren's voice. He must be on the phone. Even better, I think to myself. I can't wait to see him speechless. I tiptoe across his small living room, not letting the spikes of my heels click on the tile. His voice lingers on the other side of the door. My excitement shoots through the roof knowing he's so near.

I throw open the door to his bedroom, spot Oren, and then drop my coat bearing everything to him. My body, heart, and soul.

"Who in the hell are you?"

Like a grenade I'm blasted as a female voice asks me a question.

"Olivia," Oren steps towards me.

My vision goes to him and then to the perky blonde perched on the side of his bed.

"Who in the hell is she, Oren?"

Shock attacks me for several seconds before common sense kicks in and I snag my coat from the floor.

"Oh no, little girl. You're not leaving until you tell me who you are and what you're doing in my fiancé's house naked."

My ears buzz and head spins in confusion. Fiancé. It hurts to process the entire situation, so I run for the front door.

"Olivia." Oren's voice races after me, but I never stop or turn around.

"Olivia."

I slam the door to my car and look up to the door of Oren's place where he stands in his boxers with his sexy ruffled hair. This cannot be happening to me right now. He not only broke my heart, but also shattered it beyond repair. I guess that's what I get for opening up to him.

I fumble for my phone while backing out the complex and dial Scout's number.

"That was a world record quickie."

"Scout." My sobs take control of my speech, making it near impossible to talk.

"O, what's wrong?"

Tears blur my vision as I race away from Oren. "He...he...he has a fiancé."

"Olivia, where are you?"

"She's gorgeous and was in his room."

"Olivia, you aren't making sense. Pull over."

I panic when I'm unable to catch my breath, the tears continue to roll down my face, and that's when I try to break but it's too late as I zip through a red light. Looking to my left, the bright yellow semi-truck is the last thing I see.

"Get EMS here now." I hear a familiar voice.

I try to yell for help but only gurgle on metallic blood.

"Olivia, help is on the way."

I pry my eyes open to see Oren. I fight to get away from him.

"Stop, baby. You're hurt. You're hurt real bad."

He cradles me closer to his chest. "I'm sorry, Olivia, I'm so fucking sorry."

One of his stray tears falls onto my forearm. My stomach wretches and then streams of blood erupt from me. Then it goes black again.

Chapter 21

Just Leave

"Mr. O'Brien is here to see you again," My favorite nurse announces from the door.

My breathing tube was just taken out, leaving my throat raw. I shake my head no.

"Tell him not now," Dad replies.

"No," I barely get out. "Tell him I never want to see him."

"I know that you're hurting, Firecracker, but he saved your life."

I roll my eyes. I've heard the story a dozen times how he opened my airway on site, blah, blah, fucking blah. I wouldn't be in this bed if it weren't for his lying ass.

"You're going to have to talk to him one day." I look over to Scout in the doorway holding a large bouquet of flowers. "He sent these up. Just like he's sent flowers up every single day for the last three weeks, O. He's not going to give up."

"What?" I slam my fists into the mattress. "Am I just supposed to forgive him? He has a fiancé and used me."

Alarms go off and I know it's my oxygen levels.

"Okay, okay." Dad pats my shoulder. "Just sleep, baby girl."

That's something I can do. Close my eyes and forget the last four months of my life. I begin drifting off and hear Scout and my dad converse.

"I just wish she'd listen to him."

"You know her Scout, she's stubborn, and once hurt like this, I doubt she ever will."

"Oren deserves the right to explain himself."

"I know he does. I just don't think it will ever happen and right now she gets too worked up. She just needs to heal."

"I know," Scout agrees. "But she needs him to heal.

***

Dear Diary,

The life of a complete loser. I'm really kicking around the idea of writing my autobiography and titling it that. Yes, I've moved in with my dad, sleep on the couch because there's no way I can go in my old bedroom, and have perfected being a hermit. I have another week before I have to go back to work, which I'm dreading like no other. I'm sure my class is a wreck and my new students wild. Turning a wrench with my dad and Diesel sounds pretty damn good now.

Love, O

PS- I miss him.

Physical therapy is going well. My back is the only part killing me, but I guess with time, it will heal too. My heart, on the other hand, never will. The crisp autumn air helps kick some of the depression to the curb. Pedro loves his walks around the neighborhood bounding out on his leash.

"Pooping again? Good hell, Pedro."

Using my little baggie I scoop it up; he tugs on the leash, pulling the handle from my hand. The sound spooks him and he runs. The more he runs, the louder the handle clangs on the sidewalk.

"Pedro."

I toss the bag to the ground and try to jog as fast as I can to catch up with him, yelling his name the entire time. The leash wraps around a pole and I think it's stopped him, but the harder he pulls, he wiggles out of his Velcro harness.

"Pedro." I use my voice to get his attention. Nothing works and soon he's gone, out of sight.

I plop down on the curb and burst into tears. There goes the other love of my life.

"Olivia?" I look up to my dad in his work truck.

"Pedro just ran away." I get out between my tears.

Dad gets out of his truck, pulls me from the curb, and tucks me into the passenger seat. "Let's go home, honey."

"I lost him, Dad, I lost him." The tears stream down my face.

"He'll come back, honey."

"Or get run over or find another woman who is prettier with big ol' boobies and blonde hair."

"Olivia, you need to settle down."

"Yeah, Dad, I've lost my damn mind."

"I'll go call animal patrol and the neighbors." Dad kills the engine and runs inside. He doesn't address my craziness of losing Pedro and Oren.

I sit on the porch huddled on the front swing, crying. Dusk is beginning to settle over the city and no sign of Pedro. I'm beginning to lose hope when a cop car pulls up. I sprint down the steps and sidewalk. *What if he's dead? I can't do this.*

I don't even notice Oren standing in front of the driver door until I'm face to face with him.

"Hi Olivia."

I swallow my pride and will the tears to stay at bay. I'm sure my puffy red eyes give enough away.

When he realizes I'm not going to talk to him, he turns and opens his door.

"Here Pedro. I found your momma," Oren says into the car.

"Pedro," I squeal when Oren hands over the little fur ball to me. "You scared the shit out of me."

I look up to Oren. "Thanks."

When I turn towards the house, my dad is behind me, but I don't stay. Scurrying back up to the house, I nuzzle Pedro and will myself to forget the sight and smell of Oren. It's just another strike to my already shattered heart.

I watch through the window as Dad and Oren talk for a good thirty minutes.

"Movie tonight?" Pops asks as he walks through the front door.

"Yeah, I have it ready."

"Give me a few minutes to get out of my work clothes."

"Okay, Dad."

I stay on the couch huddled up with Pedro. I want to beat the shit out of him for running like that and I also want to hug the shit out of him. Everything inside of me wilted up at the sight of

Pedro fleeing. The fucker was off for the border, I swear.

"Popcorn?" Dad hands a teal bowl overflowing with popcorn towards me.

"No, I'm trying to quit." I wave him off while staring at him and Mom's wedding picture. "Dad, do you think you can sign me up to be a mail order bride and ship me to a foreign country."

"It doesn't work that way, honey." He sits close to me, wrapping an arm around me. I melt into his safe haven.

"I don't know how to live anymore. It sounds stupid, but I'm hurt." Tears begin rolling down my face like they always do when I attempt to talk about my feelings.

"I know you're hurting, sweetie. Mom and I had bad times, too."

"Did you lie to her about another woman?"

"No, I didn't."

"Then you don't get it at all Dad and it's not fair to compare the two."

"Your mom cried for nearly the first year of our marriage. Every night she'd roll over to face the window and cry. She wanted to go back to her family and things she knew. I tried to help her, but she had to do it in her own time. I placed an envelope of cash for her in her drawer and told her she could leave whenever she wanted to."

"But she stayed," I whisper.

"She did. We both fought to make it, never giving up on each other."

"Still not the same, Pops."

"Olivia, I need to talk to you about something."

"Oh for Christ sake's Dad, you can take me off suicide alert."

"Oren came by the shop today."

I bolt up from his chest. "Dad."

"Olivia, you will sit and listen to me."

"Dad," I warn again. "I'm already hurting enough. Why are you doing this to me?"

"Because you need to hear him out and since you won't, I'm going to tell you."

"I'm hurt enough." I cuddle back into the arm of the chair and face my dad.

"What if this helps you heal? Just listen, Olivia, and then I'll never bring it up again.

I nod and clutch a throw pillow to my chest like it even stands a chance of protecting my already shattered heart.

"Oren was engaged before he moved here. He broke it off to the dismay of his family. His parents pretty much disowned him since he wouldn't marry his high school sweetheart. Rachel was a close family friend as well."

"Don't say her name, Dad."

"Are you listening, Olivia?"

"He wasn't engaged. It had been broke off for nearly a year and Rachel came here to try to reconnect."

"Well, he was in his boxers Dad, with the shower running. Sounds like she made it happen."

"He answered the door thinking it was you and it was her. She wouldn't leave and he did his best to ignore her and then you showed up."

"Are you defending him?"

"Yes, Olivia, I am. Dammit." Dad slams the bowl of popcorn on the coffee table. Several pieces scatter across the table and topple to the beige carpet. "He's so tore up that he's leaving town, Olivia. Can't stand the fact you were hurt because of him. I've never seen a man so torn up. He's put in for a transfer and if you don't do something about it, you'll lose him forever."

Dad stands to his feet. "I know what it feels like to lose the love of your life. Oren's lost that and his family."

Chapter 22

Lost and Hurt

The last three nights have been a sleepless hell, not even the strongest pain meds able to help. My dad has given me the cold shoulder since spilling about Oren. My thoughts are so blurred with wild emotion and hurt.

I knock once on the white door. Then knock two more times before it swings open.

"Olivia." Oren's out of breath standing inside his apartment and like always, he takes my breath away. He pulls the door open wider, silently inviting me in. Boxes are scattered all over his bare apartment. Looks like he's moving on.

"I'm bringing this back to you." I open up my palm to reveal his apartment key.

"Olivia."

"Oren, don't please."

After several moments pass I set the key on his table, knowing he's not going to take it on his own.

"My dad told me everything."

"Just let me tell you how sorry I am."

"When you went back to California for that re-certification."

"I lied." He drops his head. "I went to get the rest of my things out of storage."

In a bold move, he reaches out for my arm and tugs me to the couch.

"I finally stood up for myself and left home. My transfer brought me here and I'll never regret that. Olivia, I love you and have since the first day I saw you. Please just know that." He pauses. "I know you hate me, but I'll love you forever."

"Did you go to see her in California?"

"Olivia, do you remember when I opened up about my family at the lake?"

I only nod not ready to hear the rest.

"She was part of my parent's plan. We were in love a long time ago, but it faded, it was dumb high school shit, but my parents love her. They love her looks, last name, and the fact her father is the mayor of our town. They love her. I don't and broke it off."

"Did you sleep with her when she was here?"

"Fuck no!" Oren whirls around, sending his fist through the plaster on the wall, leaving behind a huge hole. "How could you even think that Olivia?"

I stand with anger coursing through my veins. "What in the hell am I supposed to think, Oren? I show up and there's a gorgeous blonde on your bed claiming she's your fiancé. You fucking tell me!"

"She's not my fiancé, Olivia."

"You had her in your goddamn room while you were in your boxers!"

"She wouldn't leave." He raises his voice to a roar. "She's a fucking psycho."

I step up to him and thump with each word I speak. "You are a chicken shit, Oren. A fucking coward. You knew I was scared and vulnerable and you used me."

"I love you. I never used you, Olivia. You're wrong."

"I'm done here." I spin on my heels to head for the door. My palm reaches the brass knob when I feel Oren press into my back.

"You're not leaving like this again. I don't care how much you hate me right now."

"Let me go." Sobs attack my voice as the flood of tears fall.

He dips his head lower to my neck. "I'm not letting go, Olivia, ever."

"I still love you, Oren. I can't sleep or function without you."

"Will you please look at me?"

I slowly turn around until I'm facing him and my back is pressed up against the door. He clutches both sides of my face in his large palms.

"Give me another chance, please. Just sit down and let me be open about my past."

"What if I just want to love you again?" I ask with a shaky voice.

"That's all I want, baby, but please know I never cheated on you or was engaged when we started dating. That's way in my past."

"How do we move on? Also, how do we know she'll never come back?"

"I pressed harassment charges on her. She'd blow up my email, texts, and any way possible. I had plenty of evidence. Just had to swallow my pride."

"Oren, I love you. You're my first love." My voice hitches in raw emotion. "I'm going back to work and need to adjust. Please don't move, but

223

understand I need time. I'm so angry at you and the world; it's wrong and I need to find that inner peace before we can be okay."

"I'll wait for you, Olivia. Take as long as you need. I'll cancel my transfer. I'll always be here for you."

"You have to let me go now," I say with a smile through my tears.

"I'm scared, Olivia. Last time..." he trails off then his tears fall. "I went after you throwing on clothes as fast as I could. I didn't make it in time to stop you and the next thing I saw was your car tangled up in a pretzel."

"I was so messed up in the head after seeing her in your room."

"I held you in my arms praying to anyone that would listen to save you. I'll never forgive myself, Olivia, never. I was ashamed of my past and it eventually ended up hurting you."

"My actions hurt me. I should've asked questions and listened to you, but I ran and I'm never running again."

Oren drops his forehead to mine. "I'm so sorry, Olivia."

"Oren, you really are going to have to let me go."

"I can't. I don't want to. I'm scared, O."

"Trust." I peck his lips with a soft kiss. "Trust is all we are going to have from here on out. Let me go."

"Text me when you get home."

"About that..." I scrunch up my nose. "I broke my phone because my wallpaper was a goofy pic of you fishing during our camping trip. My contract is up at the end of September and I can get a new phone."

"Oh, Olivia, then call me when you get home from your landline."

"I promise."

Oren takes a tentative step back, giving me room to open the door and leave.

"I love you, Olivia."

I shut the door behind me, stepping out into the sunshine and seeing everything in a different light. My footsteps aren't so heavy, my heart not so shattered, and my soul shining with new hope.

Forgiveness is a funny creature. It takes courage to even step in the direction of it and even more strength to walk the path. If my mom could leave her homeland and find a new life here and eventually the love of her life; I can forgive, forget, and move on to something beautiful that I deserve.

HJ Bellus

Chapter 23

School Is Back In Session, Bitches

"How long are you going to make the man wait?"

I shrug, tidying up my desk and check my phone to see if Oren has texted me back yet.

"I bet he has the worse case of blue balls known to man."

"Whatever, Scout. You are worse than my dad. I swear the two of you would sell me on the black market to have Oren back in your life."

"We totally would. I mean, he sent you that new phone and flowers every Monday at work."

"He knows I need my time and has respected that. I have to fix myself before I can move on."

"It's been three months, Olivia. Hell, go to a counselor and get treatment for stripping naked in front of his ex."

"Fuck off." I toss my stapler at her.

"Two for one pizza at Jonny's tonight, you in?" she asks.

"No, I have other plans, sorry."

"Like what?" she pries.

"Like nun ya' damn beeswax."

"Fine, I'll ask Diesel."

"I knew it." I slam the top of my desk. "He's your crush."

"Fuck off, Olander."

"Oh my God, I'm right. " I throw my bag over my shoulder and walk out with Scout. "Scout and Diesel sitting in a tree…"

"Really?" She rolls her eyes.

"You're in," I taunt until she ditches me for her own car.

"Are you going straight for pizza or coming home first?"

"Pizza, why?" she asks opening the door to her car.

"Because I'm going home and putting on my coat and heels."

"About damn time, Olivia."

I know it's Oren's night off and decided it's time to jump back in. I've let the anger and fear go. Now it's time to just live. Pain is a part of living if you want to love. You can't have love without hurt or fear. I'm ready for it all.

I feed Pedro quickly and then get naked, once again conquering my fear and anxiety bundled up in the same coat with the same high heels on my feet and red lipstick on my lips.

This time I knock on his door.

"Coming," his deep voice booms from the other side. His smile instantly lights up when he sees me. "Olivia."

"Oren, I'm ready." I push him back into the apartment and step inside.

"The coat."

"Let's try this again." I tug on the collar of his polo shirt.

"I was starting to think this would never happen."

"Is anyone here?" I ask with a shy grin.

"Just my Tony the Tiger."

I glance down at the enormous bulge in his khaki shorts and then push him back until he falls down on his couch.

"School's in session." I zip down the coat and let it fall to the floor.

"Miss Olander, I've been a very naughty boy."

I straddle his lap, taking time to rub my center on the tent of his short and then kiss the piss out him. My lips attack his, leading the kiss, dipping and diving with my tongue soaking all of him up. Oren's fingers dig into the sides of my hips. He moans into my mouth when I grind down on him. I reach down and pull his shirt off, leaning back a bit, letting him toss it over the couch

"Oh, how I love you, Big O," I say with a huge smile on my face and then seal my lips back to his.

Epilogue

Dear Not So Virgin Diary,

I did it! I found the O, my Hot Cop, and happy ever after. Oren, Pedro, and I went house hunting today because that's what newlyweds do, right? That's right, maddafackas, I have a big ol' shiny diamond ring on my finger. Want to know more about the wedding? Then you'll have to read, "I Shaved My Legs For This;" it's Scout's story. Until then, may the O fairy bless you with endless orgasms and much love.

Love, Olivia O'Brien

PS-Avoid wine and vibrators...

HJ Bellus

Acknowledgments

Thank you to all the readers who always take a chance on my books. It's your support that makes my writing career possible. Thank you from the bottom of my heart.

HJ Bellus

Social Media Links

Website: www.hjbellus.com

Facebook:

https://www.facebook.com/AuthorHjBellus

Goodreads:

https://www.goodreads.com/author/show/7079478.H

_J_Bellus

Twitter: https://twitter.com/HJBellus

Keep an eye out for Scout's book!
"I Shaved My Legs For This?"

HJ Bellus

Playlist

Shower- Becky G
Sex and Candy- Marcy Playground
Baby One More Time- Britney Spears
I Want It That Way- Backstreet Boys
Hold On- Wilson Phillips
As I Lay Me Down- Sophie B. Hawkins
Genie In a Bottle- Christina Aguilera
The Freshman- Verve Pipe
I Touch Myself- Divinyls
Drive By- Train
We Found Love- Rihanna
Rehab- Amy Winehouse
Get Lucky- Draft Punk
Somewhere Over The Rainbow- Israel
Kamakawiwo'ole
Trumpets-Jason Derulo
Want to Want Me- Jason Derulo
Born This Way- Lady Gaga
Judas- Lady Gaga
You and I- Lady Gaga
The Edge of Glory- Lady Gaga
The Night Is Still Young- Nicki Minaj
FourFiveSeconds- Rihanna and Kanye West and
Paul McCartney
Take Your Time- Sam Hunt
Fast Car- Tracy Chapman
Smooth Criminal- Michael Jackson
Forever Young- Alphaville
You Get What You Give- New Radicals

HJ Bellus

Made in the USA
Middletown, DE
17 October 2016